MW01075060

Farewell to Felines

by

Kathi Daley

I want to thank the very talented Jessica Fischer for the cover art.

I so appreciate Bruce Curran, who is always ready and willing to answer my cyber questions; Jayme Maness for helping out with the book clubs; and Peggy Hyndman for helping sleuth out those pesky typos.

And, of course, thanks to the readers and bloggers in my life, who make doing what I do possible.

Thank you to Randy Ladenheim-Gil for the editing.

And a special thanks to Pam Curran, Jean Daniel, Vivian Shane, and Kristen Pfister for submitting recipes.

And finally, I want to thank my husband Ken for allowing me time to write by taking care of everything else.

Books by Kathi Daley

Come for the murder, stay for the romance.

Zoe Donovan Cozy Mystery:
Halloween Hijinks
The Trouble With Turkeys
Christmas Crazy
Cupid's Curse
Big Bunny Bump-off
Beach Blanket Barbie
Maui Madness
Derby Divas
Haunted Hamlet
Turkeys, Tuxes, and Tabbies
Christmas Cozy
Alaskan Alliance
Matrimony Meltdown
Soul Surrender
Heavenly Honeymoon
Hopscotch Homicide
Ghostly Graveyard
Santa Sleuth
Shamrock Shenanigans
Kitten Kaboodle
Costume Catastrophe
Candy Cane Caper
Holiday Hangover
Easter Escapade
Camp Carter
Trick or Treason

Reindeer Roundup
Hippity Hoppity Homicide – *March 2018*

Zimmerman Academy The New Normal
Ashton Falls Cozy Cookbook

Tj Jensen Paradise Lake Mysteries by Henery Press:
Pumpkins in Paradise
Snowmen in Paradise
Bikinis in Paradise
Christmas in Paradise
Puppies in Paradise
Halloween in Paradise
Treasure in Paradise
Fireworks in Paradise
Beaches in Paradise – *July 2018*

Whales and Tails Cozy Mystery:
Romeow and Juliet
The Mad Catter
Grimm's Furry Tail
Much Ado About Felines
Legend of Tabby Hollow
Cat of Christmas Past
A Tale of Two Tabbies
The Great Catsby
Count Catula
The Cat of Christmas Present
A Winter's Tail
The Taming of the Tabby
Frankencat
The Cat of Christmas Future
Farewell to Felines

The Cat of New Orleans – *June 2018*

Writers' Retreat Southern Seashore Mystery:
First Case
Second Look
Third Strike
Fourth Victim
Fifth Night
Sixth Cabin – *May 2018*

Rescue Alaska Paranormal Mystery:
Finding Justice
Finding Answers – *May 2018*

A Tess and Tilly Mystery:
The Christmas Letter
The Valentine Mystery
The Mother's Day Mishap – *April 2018*

Sand and Sea Hawaiian Mystery:
Murder at Dolphin Bay
Murder at Sunrise Beach
Murder at the Witching Hour
Murder at Christmas
Murder at Turtle Cove
Murder at Water's Edge
Murder at Midnight

Haunting by The Sea:
Homecoming by the Sea – *April 2018*

Seacliff High Mystery:
The Secret
The Curse

The Relic
The Conspiracy
The Grudge
The Shadow
The Haunting

Road to Christmas Romance:
Road to Christmas Past

Chapter 1

Monday, March 12

The hollow is a mystical place located in the center of Madrona Island. Given the rocky cliffs that encircle the area, it's protected from the storms that ravage the shoreline. The hollow is uninhabited except for the cats who reside in the dark spaces within the rocks. One of the things I like best about the hollow are the whispers in the air. Most believe the sound is created by the wind echoing through the canyon, but I like to think the whispers are the cats, heralding my arrival.

"Do you hear them?" I asked Tansy as we hiked to the top of the bluff that overlooked the ocean in the distance.

"No. The cats are quiet, and that worries me." Tansy has some sort of mystical power that's tied in with the magic surrounding the cats. She and her best friend, Bella, are rumored to be witches. Neither of them will confirm or deny their witchy status, but both women know things that can't be empirically explained. Tansy and I had decided to venture into the hollow after she had a premonition that the cats were unhappy and leaving the area for reasons she didn't understand.

"It's odd not to have seen a single cat by this point." I paused and looked around. "Should we continue?"

"What does your intuition tell you?"

While I don't have Tansy's powers, it does seem I've been tasked with the responsibility of working with the island's magical cats. It's not something I asked for, but I know deep in my soul that my role with the cats is tied to my destiny. "My intuition tells me we need to climb higher."

Tansy smiled and nodded for me to walk ahead of her on the narrow path. The trail was steep and covered in shale, making for a difficult and dangerous passage. I'm in pretty good shape, so I'm well equipped for a laborious hike, but I could sense a storm coming and was afraid it would arrive before Tansy and I would be able to make our way back down the trail and out of the hollow. Still, over time I've learned to trust her, so I continued, despite the risk. The trail narrowed as it wound steeply up the mountain. My legs burned as I struggled to keep my footing on the unstable ground.

"If your sense is that the cats are leaving the hollow, where are they going?" I asked. "We do live on an island, after all. It's not like they can venture very far."

"If the cats are intent on leaving they'll find a way."

I supposed Tansy was right. I knew one cat in particular who seemed to make his way between the islands with seemingly little difficulty. Of course, Ebenezer was a special cat who seemed almost human at times, but then again, all the cats I'd worked with were special in their own way.

Once we arrived at the summit, I paused to catch my breath and admire the view. The ocean looked dark and angry as the storm gathered just beyond the horizon. I listened once again, turning slightly so I was facing the sea. "My instinct tells me we should head inland, but a storm is coming and I'm not sure continuing is the best idea."

"Never doubt your instincts, Caitlin Hart."

I glanced back toward the narrow path. "I guess it couldn't hurt to go on for a bit. I'd hate to have come this far and not find out what's causing the disturbance." The detour was going to add time to our journey and I hoped it wasn't all for nothing. Usually it was Tansy who would lead the way while I followed. It felt somewhat unnatural for her to be walking behind me. I wondered if this wasn't some kind of a test to prove my worthiness to expand my role as guardian to the cats.

We had just started down the path when Tansy gasped. I stopped walking and turned around to find her holding a hand to her chest. Her long black hair blew in the wind, creating a vail of sorts that framed her pale face. "Are you okay?" I walked back the way I'd come until I was at her side.

"No. I don't think I am."

"Should we go back?"

Tansy shook her head. "I am certain we must continue."

"Are you in pain?" I didn't think going on with a sick witch was a good idea at all.

"It's the hollow that's sick. For magic to survive, a very specific balance must be maintained. I feel that balance has been altered."

I had no idea what Tansy was talking about, but a bit of color had returned to her normally pale complexion that made me feel better. "Are you sure you want to continue?"

"I'm sure."

I took a deep breath and turned back to the narrow path. "Okay. But let me know if you need to stop."

I walked down the trail slowly so as not to tax Tansy, but to be honest, the farther I traveled, the more urgent was my desire to run. "There's a fork," I said after we'd been walking a while. "Both paths are narrow and both continue inland."

"Close your eyes and focus on the paths ahead of you," Tansy suggested.

I did as she instructed.

"Which path feels right to you?"

"The trail to the left," I said with a confidence I wasn't really feeling.

"All right. Then we'll continue to the left."

I nodded and headed down that trail. I could feel Tansy walking behind me, but I could also sense her distress. I stopped and turned around. "I can go on alone if you want to wait for me here."

"No. We're close. Can you smell it?"

I took a deep breath and wrinkled my nose at the stench. "What is it?"

"The source of the disturbance. It won't be long now."

"Until what?" I had to ask. This whole thing was beginning to freak me out. After several years of witnessing some truly spectacular things, there's no way I was going to try to argue that magic didn't exist, but the idea that it depended on some sort of perfect balance was a bit hard to swallow.

"There." I turned around in time to see Tansy pointing to a small body of water in the distance.

After we'd traversed the space between where we'd stood and the small pond, I looked down at the murky surface of the usually pristine blue water. "Something's wrong with the water. It smells awful. I think it's been contaminated."

Tansy frowned. "Yes, I'm afraid it has been tainted. I imagine the lack of clean water is the catalyst that's driving the cats away."

"How can we fix it?"

"I sense the tainted water is a symptom of a larger problem. The answers we seek will reveal themselves in the coming days. We've done what we can for now."

I turned and headed back in the direction from which we had come. As we neared the top of the path and the bluff, I heard thunder rumbling in the distance. I glanced out at the dark sea as we paused momentarily before continuing down the other side. The dark clouds had completely blocked the light the sun would have provided. I just hoped we'd make it back to the car before the worst of the storm hit.

"Do you think the cats will return if we can find the source of the contamination and fix it?"

"Perhaps."

The walk down from the summit was accomplished much more quickly than the trip up.

When we arrived at my car I noticed a large brown cat with bright eyes and pointy ears sitting on the hood. "Am I to assume this cat will be leaving with us?"

"Apollo is here to help."

"With the water in the hollow?"

Tansy picked up the cat. She closed her eyes and whispered to it in a language I didn't understand. The cat meowed a couple of times, and Tansy opened her eyes. "I'm afraid Apollo is here to help you resolve a different issue. Follow his lead and you'll find the answers you seek."

"Has someone died?"

Tansy nodded but didn't answer. My heart sank. Occasionally, cats appeared to help me deal with a problem other than a murder, but most of the time when one of them appeared someone had died. I wondered who.

As we drove back to Pelican Bay, where Tansy lived with Bella, the sky continued to darken. The wind had picked up quite a bit, and I could tell by the heaviness of the clouds that we were in for a serious storm. I dropped Tansy at her house, then drove back toward the peninsula, where I lived. I was nearing the point where I turned on to the peninsula road when Apollo started meowing and jumping around the car. I slowed and eventually pulled over.

"What is it? Are you trying to tell me who's died?"

"Meow." Apollo began pawing at the glove box. I opened it, and a sheet of yellow paper fell out of it and onto the floor.

"That's just the program from Sunday services at St. Patrick's."

Apollo jumped from the front seat onto the floor. He picked up the paper in his mouth, then leaped back onto the seat. Once he was settled he placed the program on the seat between us.

"I don't understand what you want me to do. Today is Monday. Services are on Sundays."

"Meow." Apollo placed his paw on the program.

I looked at what he seemed to be pointing to. "That's the set list the adult choir sang during yesterday's service. Do you want me to go to St. Patrick's?"

The cat didn't respond.

I tried to figure out exactly what it was the cat was pointing to. "Do you want me to pay a visit to Father Bartholomew? Oh God, he isn't the one who died, is he?"

The cat still didn't respond.

"It isn't Sister Mary?" My heart began to race as the thought entered my mind. I'd known Sister Mary for most of my life. She was my best friend's biological mother and almost a member of my family. "Please tell me it isn't Sister Mary."

Apollo just stared. I'm not sure if cats can experience frustration, but I got the feeling this one was quickly becoming impatient with me. It seemed his silence represented a negative response, so I continued to guess at what it was he was trying to tell me. "Maybe someone whose name is on the list?"

"Meow."

"Okay, good. Now we're getting somewhere." The first name on the list was Thea Blane, the new director of the adult choir. "Do you want me to pay a visit to Thea?"

"Meow."

"Is Thea the one who's died?"

"Meow."

I closed my eyes and offered a silent prayer. She and I hadn't been close, but I'd known her casually for quite a few years. She was single, lived alone, and didn't seem to have any family on the island. Still, I was sure there were those who would mourn her passing. I looked at the darkening sky. Thea lived all the way over in Harthaven and the storm was getting closer. If I continued to her place, we risked getting caught in it. "Are you sure Thea's the one we need to find?"

"Meow."

I glanced at the sky one last time. It would be a risk to make the trip, but I couldn't go on the off chance Thea was still alive and Apollo's insistence was to save her, not simply to discover her remains. Making a decision, I pulled back onto the road and headed toward Harthaven.

When Apollo and I arrived at Thea's place I saw her car in the driveway. I still hoped she was alive and Apollo had brought us here for another reason. Once again, I prayed we weren't too late. I opened my door, which allowed Apollo to slip out of the car before I could stop him. I watched as he went to the door, then joined him on the front porch, rang the bell, and waited. My heart was pounding the entire time. I waited another minute before ringing the bell for a second time. When Thea still didn't answer, I knocked on the door and called her name. When she still didn't answer I tried to turn the knob. The door was locked.

"Maybe I should call Finn," I said as the first raindrops began to fall. "Come to think of it, maybe that's what I should have done in the first place."

"Meow." Apollo hopped off the raised porch and ran around to the back of the house.

I pulled the hood of my sweatshirt over my hair and followed him as the rain increased in intensity. At the side of the house, I found the wooden gate leading to the backyard open slightly. Apollo slipped inside and out of sight. I felt I had no choice but to follow, so I lowered my head and trotted to the gate. When I reached the back door I saw it was ajar, and Apollo was nowhere in sight. I opened the door wider, calling Thea as I did so.

I walked through the kitchen to the main living area of the house. "Thea," I called once again. "It's Caitlin Hart. Are you home?"

My words were met with silence. I looked around for the cat and spotted him sitting on top of a small desk against the wall near the foot of the stairs. When he saw I'd found him, the cat jumped down and ran up the stairs. As I followed, I heard the first rumbling of thunder in the distance.

At the top of the stairs was a short hallway that led to four rooms. The first contained a bed and a dresser and looked like a guest room. It appeared to be empty and undisturbed, so I continued to the second room, which turned out to be a bathroom. The third room looked a lot like one of the rooms in my Aunt Maggie's house that she used for a craft and sewing room, so I imagined the last door would lead to the master bedroom. When I saw a pair of feet sticking out from the far side of the bed I knew for certain what I had feared since Apollo had snuck into the house was true. Thea Blane was dead.

Chapter 2

"Who would want to kill Thea?" My best friend, Tara O'Brian, asked later that evening. She, along with my fiancé, Cody West, my brother, Danny Hart, and my sister, Siobhan Finnegan, were sitting in my oceanfront cabin discussing the events of the day.

"I don't know," I answered. "I didn't know Thea well, but based on the interactions we'd had, I found her to be pleasant."

"Are you planning to look in to her death?" Danny asked.

I wasn't a cop or a private investigator, but I seemed to be pulled into many of the unusual deaths that occurred on the island. I glanced toward Apollo, who was curled up on a chair next to the fire Cody had built when he arrived. "It seems I'm meant to participate in the investigation of Thea's death in some way because Apollo found me and then led me to her body. Maybe Finn will know more when he gets here."

Ryan Finnegan, Finn for short, was the island's resident deputy and Siobhan's husband. I'd called him right after I found Thea's body. He'd arrived shortly after my call and was still there as far as I knew.

"I'm totally in to help you in any way I can," Tara volunteered.

"I'm in as well," Danny added. "My boat's leased until the end of April, so I'm looking for something to do until then."

Danny lived on his boat and operated a whale watch tour in the summer. During the winter he usually leased the boat and moved in with our Aunt Maggie to save money. Of course, now that Maggie was making plans to marry the love of her life, Michael Killian, the former priest at St. Patrick's who had recently retired and left the priesthood, it might not work out for Danny to crash with her whenever the mood struck him. Although Maggie had been out of town a lot as of late. I guess I could see why Maggie and Michael might not want to explore their new relationship under the watchful eyes of his former parishioners.

"I think we need the whiteboard," Siobhan announced. She and Finn were also living with my aunt this winter and was by far the most organized of the five Hart siblings.

"I'll run over to get it for you," Danny offered.

"It's pouring rain," I pointed out. "We can just take notes on a pad of paper and transfer them to the whiteboard when the rain lets up."

"Okay. I'll call Finn to tell him to come over here when he's done," Siobhan said, rubbing her pregnant belly just as a loud clap of thunder shook the cabin.

"I hope the peninsula road doesn't flood," Tara said once the rumbling had come to an end.

"You're welcome to stay here tonight if you want," I offered. My cabin had only one bedroom, but the sofa pulled out into a bed.

"There are free rooms at Maggie's now that Aiden, Mom, and Cassie, have moved out," Siobhan said.

My oldest brother, Aiden, had been staying with Maggie while he recovered from an auto accident he'd been involved in just before Christmas, and Mom and our youngest sister had been staying with Maggie while their condo was undergoing repairs, but all three were back in their own homes now.

"Maybe I'll call my neighbor and have her feed Bandit," Tara answered, referring to her cat. "I do hate driving in weather like this."

Cody put another log on the fire while Tara made her call and Siobhan spoke to Finn. Then we gathered around my dining table to come up with a strategy for investigating Thea's death.

"First off, was there any evidence that she was murdered rather than suffering a natural event such as a heart attack?" Siobhan asked.

"Yes," I confirmed. "There was a large gash on the back of her head, which I suspect will turn out to be the cause of death. I think the most relevant question at this point will be who had a reason to want Thea dead."

"I'm not sure a choir dispute would constitute a motive for murder, but Thea did beat Pam Wilkins out for the position of director for the adult choir," Tara started off.

"Pam was furious," Siobhan agreed. "She's been telling everyone that Thea basically stole the position from her by spreading vicious lies about her."

I hesitated and then responded. "Pam was upset about losing out on the role she felt should have been hers, but murder? It seems sort of harsh."

"I don't disagree, but I thought the point was to get names on a list," Tara countered.

"You're right." I glanced at Siobhan and told her to go ahead and add Pam to the list she had started on a yellow legal pad. "As long as you're at it, add Victoria Grace. She was upset when Thea started dating her ex-husband. In fact, she went as far as to suggest Thea was responsible for their marriage breaking up in the first place, although to be fair, I don't think that's true. If you ask me, Victoria nagged the poor man to the point that he decided he couldn't live with the constant ridicule."

Danny chuckled. "I remember when Ethan came into the bar and announced he was leaving Victoria once and for all. Everyone in the place stood up and applauded. Most of the folks at O'Malley's that night felt Ethan had stayed in the marriage a lot longer than he should have."

"Jealousy is generally a good motive for murder and Thea was a beautiful woman," Tara added. "I know quite a few women on the island weren't happy when they found out Thea was going to be temping in the offices where their husbands worked."

"Who else should we speak to?" I asked.

Everyone fell silent. I glanced at Apollo, who was sleeping on the sofa next to my dog, Max. If history served as a guide, the secret to finding Thea's killer lay with the cat. The problem was, the cat wasn't exhibiting any interest in our conversation.

"What about Lilly Kent?" Siobhan suggested.

Lilly was currently dating Thea's ex-husband, Steve. Thea and Steve Blane had been divorced for quite some time, but the two had remained friends, and it had been rumored Lilly wasn't thrilled with the amount of time they continued to spend together.

"It would be pretty extreme for Lilly to plan to kill Thea to get her out of the way, but it's possible the two of them may have been talking and, in the heat of the moment, Lilly could have hit Thea." I had Siobhan add her to the list.

Danny got up from the table and wandered over to the large picture window that looked out at the sea. "The rain has really picked up and the water looks about as angry as I've ever seen it."

"I wish Finn was back." Siobhan looked worried. "I hate that he's driving around in this stuff."

"Finn's a smart guy," I tried to reassure my older sister. "I'm sure he'll pull over to the side of the road if the rain gets too intense."

We all jumped when a crack of thunder rattled the windows in my cabin. I looked out toward the sea. The waves, which normally rolled gently onto the shore on this part of the island, had increased in size to the point where the surge had inched up to within a few yards of my beachside deck.

"Do you think we're safe here?" Tara asked.

"I think so," I answered. "This cabin has stood in this spot for more than five decades. We've had storms as bad as this, if not worse. I think we'll be fine." I glanced at Siobhan. "I do wish Finn was here, however."

"I'll call him again," Siobhan said as a flash of lightning exploded overhead. The lights flickered before coming back on. It looked like we might lose power by the end of the evening.

Max, who was normally not all that affected by thunder and lightning, hopped off the sofa and wandered over to where I was sitting. I spoke softly to him, letting him know everything would be okay. He seemed pacified by my words, but he still curled up at my feet rather than returning to the sofa.

"That cat hasn't moved in an hour, despite all the noise. Are we sure it's alive?" Danny chuckled. I could tell he was kidding, but it did seem odd that the cat hadn't reacted at all to the storm.

"I noticed his tail moved a couple of times." Tara smiled.

"I guess he wants to rest until it's time for him to do his thing." I glanced at Siobhan, who had just hung up after speaking to Finn. "Is he okay?"

"He's on his way. He said he'd be here in about five minutes. The power is out in Harthaven. So far, this end of the island still has electricity, but he thought we should gather candles and flashlights. He suggested we all move up to the main house. With Maggie away, there are plenty of guest rooms for everyone, and he felt it would be a good idea to be farther away from the water."

I glanced at Cody, who shrugged. "Okay," I answered. "He's probably right. Let's all stay at Maggie's. Just give me a minute to grab a few things."

Danny helped Siobhan navigate the path across the lawn toward the main house, while Tara followed along behind. I grabbed my bag and called to Max, and Cody picked up Apollo. The fire had burned down to the point where it should be fine unattended, so Cody and I, along with the animals, made a mad dash through the rain. When we arrived at Maggie's, wet but safe, we joined the others, who were in the living room.

"Do you think Mr. Parsons is okay?" I asked Cody, mentioning the elderly man he lived with and cared for.

"He should be fine. I planned to spend the night with you, so Banjo and Summer were staying over with him." Banjo and Summer were a hippy couple who lived down the beach and often stayed with Mr. Parsons and his dog, Rambler, when Cody wasn't home.

"That's good. They're probably better off with him anyway. Their place tends to flood when there's a strong storm surge."

"Danny, why don't you run upstairs and grab the whiteboard?" Siobhan said. "We may as well use it as long as we're here and the lights are still on."

I heard Finn's car in the drive just as Danny was returning with the whiteboard. I was glad we were all together for the storm. Being so close to the sea, there was always the possibility of things getting bad really fast, and it was good to have Finn home.

Once he had the chance to change out of his wet clothes, we picked up the conversation where we'd left off. We'd put Pam Wilkins, Victoria Grace, and Lilly Kent, on the board, even though we all agreed none of them were probably responsible for Thea's death.

"Did you find anything at the crime scene?" I asked Finn.

"While I'll need to wait for the medical examiner's report to be certain, it appears Thea died due to blunt force trauma to the back of her head. There's evidence of an altercation; it appears she'd been arguing with someone and had turned, probably to walk away, when she was struck from behind. We didn't find the murder weapon and are assuming the killer took it with them. We found some fingerprints, as well as hair and some red fibers, but we aren't sure if they belong to Thea, her killer, or some random person. I plan to canvas the neighborhood tomorrow to speak to her neighbors. With the storm accelerating in intensity, I decided it was best to get back to the peninsula while I still could. It looks like you've started a murder board."

Siobhan caught him up with the reasons we'd added each of the three suspects. Finn thought it was unlikely any of the three was the killer but agreed it was best to speak to as many people as we could come up with.

The lightning had started up again, and Max came over to put his head in my lap; he really didn't like all the racket. Apollo was curled up in Maggie's chair near the fire with her two house cats and seemed as content as he'd been all evening. I began to scratch Max behind the ears, hoping to distract him from the rumbling in the distance.

"We should find out where Thea was temping this past week," Cody suggested. "I still think it's feasible her death could be related to her job."

"What do you mean, related to her job?" Tara asked.

"Maybe she was temping for an attorney and came across sensitive information she wasn't meant to see," Cody answered. "Maybe the information was so sensitive, the subject of the information wanted to be sure she didn't have the opportunity to tell anyone else."

"What sort of information could be that sensitive?" Tara asked.

"Something illegal, for example. Although there are other jobs that could lead to a person discovering something they're better off not knowing. Thea could have been temping with a cleaning service and might have overheard something while cleaning a home or office. I'm not saying her death is definitely related to her job, but I think it's worth looking in to."

"Okay," I said. "Just put down *temp job* as the suspect or person of interest on the list for now. When we find out where she was temping, we'll know who to talk to."

"What about a spurned lover?" Siobhan asked. "Thea was a beautiful woman and we know she liked to play the field. Maybe someone she was dating became overly serious and felt slighted when she moved on to the next man."

"John Walkman," Danny said. "He dated Thea for a couple of months until she broke it off. I ran into John about a week ago at O'Malley's, and he was complaining to anyone who would listen that she was about as coldhearted as they come."

Siobhan added his name on the whiteboard.

"I'm not saying she's a suspect, but Thea was good friends with Kim Pemberton. Someone should have a chat with her," Tara suggested. "She might know something about her life only a close friend would."

"That's a good idea. I'll talk to her tomorrow," Finn said.

"It shouldn't be you," Siobhan countered. "If she knows something juicy, especially something that might put Thea in a bad light, she might not be willing to tell someone interviewing her in an official capacity."

"I'll talk to her," I offered. "And I'll talk to Lilly Kent and Pam Wilkins too. Danny, you talk to John Walkman because you know him the best. Finn can follow up with the crime scene guys and the medical examiner. We'll all meet back here tomorrow and come up with a strategy based on what we find out."

"What about Victoria Grace?" Tara asked.

"I'll talk to her," Siobhan said. "I'll also see if I can find out where Thea was temping last week."

I figured we had a good place to start, and it was nice to have the sleuthing gang together again. I was about to suggest we find something for dessert when a loud crash of thunder made the house vibrate, followed by flickering lights and then complete darkness.

Chapter 3

Tuesday, March 13

A quick glance out the window the following morning confirmed that the rain had settled in for a good long stay. At least the wind had died down and the power was back on. Cody needed to get to the newspaper early, so we both headed back to my cabin to shower and get ready for the day. Siobhan, who'd been eating breakfast at the dining table when I went downstairs, informed me that Tara had already started out for home, and Finn had gone to work early to deal with storm-related emergency calls.

Cody suggested I just ride into town with him, but he wanted to check on Mr. Parsons before going to work. I needed to see to the cats in the sanctuary before leaving for the day, so he planned to come back for me and the cats I was bringing to the lounge in Coffee Cat Books on his way to the newspaper office.

The Harthaven Cat Sanctuary was founded by my aunt Maggie when our previous mayor pushed through a law allowing the residents of Madrona Island to remove the feral cats from their property by any means they chose. Many of them just ignored the cats that had roamed freely for as long as anyone could remember, while others trapped them and brought them to the sanctuary. There were a few islanders who chose to use more lethal means of removing the cats under Mayor Bradley's reign of terror, but since Siobhan had taken over as mayor following his death, use of violence to remove the animals was once again a punishable offense.

It seemed to me the number of cats we housed had decreased significantly, due in part to the spay and neuter program Maggie and I had been committed to for the past several years. In addition to reducing the number of wild kittens born each year, the presence of the cats in our cat lounge had increased our adoption rate significantly.

"Good morning, Moose," I said to one of our ornerier full-time residents. "I hope you made it through the worst of the storm okay."

The big cat hissed at me.

"I have salmon treats this morning," I bribed, holding out my hand.

Moose looked at it with suspicion before taking it from me and running to a corner at the far side of his pen to eat it. I left food for him, then cleaned his litter box before moving on to the next pen, which housed a group of cats with more agreeable dispositions. I normally brought four cats with me to the store every day, so I selected the ones for today while I cleaned the pen. I tried to rotate them so everyone had a chance to meet customers interested in adoption, but it was the kittens that seemed to find homes the fastest.

After everyone was fed and the entire place cleaned and aired out, I went back to the cabin to wash up and wait for Cody. With all the rain we were having, it looked like it would be a slow day at the bookstore. Coffee Cat Books depended on traffic from the ferry, and when the weather was bad fewer people made the trip out to the island.

I checked my phone to see I had a message from Tara. She'd called to let me know she'd stopped by the bookstore to check on things on her way home and found the roof over the cat lounge had leaked. She suggested we close for the day so the workmen could make the repairs before any more damage was done. I called her back and agreed closing made sense. Not only did it look like we were in for at least another twelve hours of rain, but according to the local forecast, the wind was supposed to pick up again later in the afternoon.

I called Cody to let him know I wasn't going in to work but still wanted to go to town to begin our investigation. He still thought it was a good idea for me to ride in with him because my car was so temperamental. I could drop him off at the newspaper and use his truck to make my stops.

"I hear we're supposed to get another two to three inches of rain today," Cody said as we carefully made our way along the partially flooded peninsula road.

"We should stop at the market to pick up whatever we need just in case the road floods and we can't get out for a few days. Are Banjo and Summer planning to stay with Mr. Parsons again?"

"I spoke with them this morning and they agreed to stay with him until the storm passes. For one thing, his home is much safer than the hut they live in. If Tara plans to come back for the sleuthing meeting tonight she should plan to stay over. Based on the weather report, the worst of the storm is supposed to hit at around six o'clock this evening."

"We should be sure to get back to the peninsula by then."

"I have some things to do this morning, but I should be free by lunch."

After dropping Cody at the newspaper I headed to Shells and Sunshine, the souvenir shop Pam Wilkins owned and operated. I wasn't sure if she'd be open on a day like this, but it wouldn't hurt to head to Harthaven in any case. My mom and Cassie lived in a condo there, and I wanted to check in with them to make sure they had everything they needed if they had to wait out the storm.

Pam had been singing in the adult choir at St. Patrick's since I was a child. Thea had been a member of the church for at least as long but had only joined the choir about five years ago. When the woman who had been directing the choir for the past twenty years stepped down, it seemed no one was interested in taking her place, but after at least a month without a director, Pam had stepped up and said she would do it, which seemed to have prompted Thea to put her name in for it as well. Both women were interviewed, and in the end, Thea was chosen over Pam. I could see why the decision might have angered Pam, although I didn't think she would go so far as to kill Thea over it. Still, she was on our list of people to interview, so I may as well talk to her.

"Afternoon, Pam," I greeted her as I walked through the door to her shop. "I wasn't sure you would be open today with all the rain."

"I came in to do some paperwork I need to get to the accountant today, but I haven't had a single customer all morning, so I'm thinking about going home and settling in with a cup of hot tea and the trashy romance novel I recently purchased."

"It does seem like a good day to snuggle in by the fire. It's just sprinkling now, but I hear the rain is supposed to pick up by noon, and then the storm is supposed to intensify by dinnertime."

"I guess I will go ahead and close, then. There's no use sitting here by myself all day. Can I get you anything before I turn off the cash register?"

"Actually, the reason I'm here is to talk to you about Thea Blane."

"Thea and I are no longer friends, so I doubt I can provide any information you might be looking for regarding her."

I hesitated, unsure how to break the news that Thea was dead. "It sounds as if you haven't heard about Thea. I don't suppose a lot of people have. I hate to be the bearer of bad news, but I'm afraid she's dead."

Pam's mouth fell open. Based on the shocked expression on her face, I felt she hadn't been the one to kill her.

"Dead? How did she die? And when?" Pam asked.

"I found her body yesterday. I don't know exactly when she died, but it appeared to me that she'd been gone for at least a day or two."

Pam's eyes grew big as the news really hit her. "You know, she wasn't at church on Sunday. I thought it was odd that she hadn't even bothered to call to let anyone know she was unable to attend, given the fact that she had the choir to lead and a solo to sing."

"Had Thea said anything to you that might explain her death?"

Pam shook her head. "Like I said, we aren't friends anymore. I haven't had a conversation with her since she basically stole the role of choir director right out from under me."

"When was the last time you saw her?"

"She was at choir practice on Tuesday of last week. Normally, we practice on Tuesday and Thursday, but there was an evening activity at the elementary school that quite a few of the choir members wanted to attend, so the Thursday practice was canceled. And then, like I said, she didn't show up for service on Sunday."

"Do you happen to know where Thea has been temping?"

Pam shook her head. "Again, she and I were no longer friends. We don't talk like we once did. I do know she'd been moving around quite a bit lately. She mentioned to the choir that she might miss the Thursday practice several weeks ago because she was working for an accounting firm that was open late on Thursdays during tax season. I don't know if she was still with them or not. You might ask Kim Pemberton. They were friends. I know they had lunch a couple of times a week."

"I planned to speak to Kim this afternoon. Can you think of anyone else Thea was close to?" I asked.

"I know she volunteered at the library, so you might talk to Gigi Smith. And I saw her at O'Malley's with Jared Pitman last week. I don't know for certain they were on a date, but they seemed chummy. Of course, Thea was the sort to be chummy with a lot of men, if you know what I mean."

"I do and thank you. I'll speak to both of them. If you hear anything or think of anything else, please call me."

"I will. I've been furious with Thea ever since the choir fiasco, but I'm sorry to hear she passed. Do you suspect foul play?"

"While I haven't had confirmation of cause of death, that's what Finn suspects."

"If someone hurt her, I hope you find out who it was and make them pay."

I left Pam's store and went to check on Mom and Cassie. Their condo was inland from the sea, so I wasn't really worried about storm surge in their case, but I wanted to be sure they had all the supplies they'd need should the storm intensify. When I arrived I found Cassie home alone.

"Gabe came by and took Mom to the store," Cassie said. Gabe Williams was my mom's boyfriend, although it felt strange for me to refer to anyone as *Mom's boyfriend.* My mom and Gabe, a widower, seemed to be moving toward a long-term arrangement and I wouldn't be surprised to find them married after Cassie headed off to college in the fall.

"I'm glad. I know Mom doesn't like to drive in the rain, so I wanted to be sure the two of you had what you needed before the storm got worse." I glanced at the kitchen table. "It looks like you've been researching colleges again."

Cassie sighed, then let out a long groan. I could sense her frustration. "I need to make a decision about where to go by the end of the month. Even though I've done a ton of research I can't seem to commit. One college has a better academic program, while another has a better location. And then, when I factor in things like where my friends are going or how close to home I'll be, the whole thing seems overwhelming. I wish there was a clear choice."

"I'm sure you'll figure it out. If push comes to shove, you can always flip a coin," I teased.

"It might come down to that. I've even considered staying here on the island and getting a job."

"I think you'll be happy to have a degree in the long run."

Cassie lifted a brow. "Really? You didn't go to college. Aiden didn't go to college. And Danny didn't go to college. In fact, only Siobhan has a degree."

"That's true. But these days a college degree can open doors that will be closed to you any other way."

Cassie leaned a hip on the corner of the sofa. "Are you happy?"

I narrowed my gaze. "What do you mean?"

"Happy. Are you generally satisfied with your life and the direction it's taken?"

"Yes, of course I'm happy."

"Have you ever once found yourself wishing you'd left the island and gone to college?"

I took a deep breath. "No," I admitted. "But I'm a homebody. It never occurred to me to leave after high school. I can't imagine living anywhere else." I paused. "Are you serious about not wanting to go to college?"

Cassie shrugged. "Maybe. I'd be a lot more serious about it if I didn't feel like my not going would ruin Mom's plans."

I sat down on the edge of the sofa. "What do you mean, ruin her plans?"

Cassie sat down next to me. "When you graduated high school, Aunt Maggie remodeled the summer cabin so you could stay on the island and move out of the house. My problem is, I know Mom and Gabe are just waiting for me to head off to college so they can move in together. They haven't said as much, but I can tell that's what they're thinking by reading between the lines of other things they've said. I know Mom's been somewhat discontented since the house burned down and Aiden moved out. I want her to be happy, and it seems the only way for her to be that way is for me to go to college, freeing her from any obligation she might feel toward me."

I took Cassie's hand in mine. "I'm not going to tell you what to do. This is a decision you need to make yourself. But going to college so Mom can marry Gabe shouldn't be your only reason to go. If you decide, after taking everything into account, that you don't want to go away to school, we'll figure something out. Tara has an extra room I suspect she'd be happy to rent to you temporarily, and when Cody and I get married I'll be moving in with him and the cabin will be free. I can't speak for Maggie, but I don't see why she'd mind if you moved in after I moved out."

Cassie smiled and hugged me. "Thanks, Cait. I have a lot more thinking to do, but it helps knowing I have options if I decide to stay."

I hugged Cassie back hard, then pulled away slightly. "Do you have any idea what you might want to do if you did stay?"

"No, and that's part of the problem. It's not like I have a grand plan for my life. I'll need to take some time to really figure it out."

"It's hard. I didn't have a grand plan after high school either. In fact, I pretty much just floated around from one job to another until Tara and I came up with the idea for the bookstore."

"Speaking of the bookstore, why aren't you there? Is it closed today?"

"Leaky roof. Tara has someone coming out to fix it, but I wouldn't want to be out fixing a roof on a day like today."

Cassie glanced out the window. "It seems like the rain is tapering off."

"It is, temporarily. It's supposed to get bad later." I grabbed a bottle of water from the refrigerator. "I should be going. I have quite a few errands to take care of before the next wave of the storm makes landfall. Tell Mom I stopped by, and if you want to talk, call me. I'm always here for you."

"Thanks, Cait. If the bookstore is open tomorrow and school's canceled again, let Tara know I'd be happy to come in. I could use a boost to my currently nonexistent income."

"I'll tell her. And I know you feel pressured to make a decision right now, but take the time you need to make one you can live with."

I left the condo and headed to the library. Again, I wasn't sure it would be open with the storm, but the rain had slowed to a drizzle and the wind had temporarily stopped, so I imagined it would try to stay open. Gigi Smith had started working at the library the previous fall, so I didn't know her well. Given that Tara and I owned a bookstore, we usually had a lot of interaction with the staff and volunteers, but between the two of us, Tara tended to be the one to read a lot of different types of novels and so was the one more likely to interact with other readers in the community.

Luckily, when I arrived at the library I found it open. I went inside to find Gigi at the circulation desk.

"I wasn't sure you'd be open with the storm and all," I greeted the young blonde with huge curls trailing down her back.

"We plan to close by three o'clock so the staff can get home before the next wave of the storm hits. Is the bookstore open today?"

I shook my head. "Leaky roof over the cat lounge."

"It's a good thing the leak isn't over the books and your other inventory."

"It's a really good thing. Listen, I don't have a lot of time to chat, but I wanted to ask you about Thea Blane. I understand she volunteered here."

"She does. Normally she's here on Mondays and Wednesdays, but she didn't show yesterday. I tried to get her on the phone but there was no answer and she never returned my message. Are you looking for her?"

"No. I'm afraid Thea has passed away."

"She's dead? When did that happen?"

"I don't know exactly when she died, but I found her body yesterday. Do you happen to know what her plans were for this past weekend?"

"I know she had a job on Saturday. She didn't say exactly what she was doing or where. She just said she'd see me in church on Sunday, but I didn't see her, and one of our regulars confirmed she never showed. How did she die?"

"Honestly, I don't know the specifics, but I suspect foul play. Did she say anything to you that might explain why someone would want her dead?"

Gigi hesitated. I waited for her to answer. "I don't know who would want to kill Thea or why, but I did have a rather odd conversation with her last week. She asked me if we had any books about legal codes in this county. Our legal section is pretty thin, so I suggested she talk to Paul Gibson if she had a legal question. He's a member of one of our book clubs, and I knew Thea and Paul had met."

"And she didn't give you any idea what information she needed?"

"No, she didn't. I wondered that myself, but a customer walked up, interrupting our conversation, and we never got back to it. You could ask Paul if she ever followed up with him."

"Yeah, I will. Before I go, can you think of anyone else who might have a grudge against Thea? Anyone at all with a motive to want her dead?"

Gigi crossed her arms over her chest. She tilted her head just a bit so that her long curls brushed the counter in front of her. I watched as several emotions crossed her face. Eventually, she began to speak. "I liked Thea. She was an interesting person and a hard worker who seemed to be willing to do anything. Having said that, I came to learn that not everyone felt the same way about her. She looked at the world as her oyster. If she saw something she wanted, she took it. Don't get me wrong: She was willing to do what it took to get what she wanted, but she didn't seem to notice the others who might be in her path. I guess you heard about the choir fiasco with Pam Wilkins?"

"I did."

"And I know of at least three women who made it clear to me that they'd only attend events when Thea wouldn't be present after getting into some sort of feud with her over one thing or another. The thing is, while the women Thea wronged held on to their grudges, it seemed to me that she forgot all about them and moved on within days of whatever disagreement had caused the rift in the first place. I'm honestly not even sure she understood she'd done irreparable damage to her relationships."

"Thea did seem to have a way of thinking things weren't a big deal when they very much were. Can you give me the names of anyone you can think of with a grudge, no matter how small? If I hit a dead end I may follow up with the people from the list."

By the time I finished speaking to Gigi it was lunchtime, so I went to the newspaper to check in with Cody. He was just finishing up for the day, so he said he could go with me to talk with Thea's friend, Kim Pemberton. She worked at a dentist's office in Harthaven, so we decided to grab some lunch first at one of our favorite sandwich places on the pier.

We ordered our food and found a table near a window. It had started to rain harder, and from the dark, heavy clouds on the horizon, I had no doubt we were in for a lot more before the storm passed entirely.

"So, I have some interesting news," Cody said after our sandwiches had been delivered.

"Interesting good or interesting bad?" I asked.

"I'm not sure how you'll feel about it, but I'd say interesting good. I got a call from the man who schedules guests on a local morning show produced by an independent television station in New Orleans. He wondered if I'd be willing to discuss my SEAL training program on the show sometime in the next few months. I told him that I'd only be able to discuss material approved by the oversight committee I'm working with, which he thought would be fine. He's planning to do a segment every Wednesday in April and May on some aspect of the armed services and thought my work with the SEALs, combined with my background, would be of interest to their viewers."

"Are you going to do it?"

"I need to call him back to let him know one way or the other by the end of the week. I spoke to my contact at the base in Orlando who said he'd run it by his superiors, but he felt it would be fine for me to be a guest as long as the topics that could and couldn't be discuss were worked out ahead of time. We never did manage to take the trip we planned in January, so I thought maybe you could come with me and we could make a short vacation of it."

I set my sandwich down and took a sip of my water. "I've always wanted to visit New Orleans; it's on my list of top-ten places to see. As long as we make the trip before Memorial Day, Tara shouldn't have a problem with my taking time off. Willow's baby is due in April and Siobhan's in June, so a trip in May would be perfect."

"Okay, I'll see what I can work out. The weather should be nice in that part of the country in May as well."

We finished eating, then headed to the office where Kim Pemberton worked. She was alone in the reception area when we got there. She'd heard about Thea's death and was heartbroken that her friend had died in what looked to have been a violent manner.

"The dentist and hygienist are both off, so I'm in the office alone today. I'm free to talk if I can help in any way," Kim informed us. "Of course, if the phone rings, I'll need to answer it."

"That won't be a problem at all," I replied. "I imagine Finn will be by to speak with you too at some point. I'm wondering if you know anything that would explain what happened to Thea."

"I can't imagine why anyone would want to kill her. She did have a way of getting under the skin of some of the people she interacted with, but I don't think she made anyone mad enough to attack her."

"Do you remember the last time you spoke to her?"

"Friday. She called me to say she had some things to take care of for her most recent temp job, so she needed to cancel lunch on Saturday."

"Do you know who she was temping for?"

"I think it was the real estate office in Pelican Bay. She temped here for two weeks when I was visiting my sister in Portland, and then she worked for that photo shop down by the wharf. I think that gig was only for a weekend, so she may have started at the real estate office on Monday; I'm not sure. I worked a lot of extra hours last week, trying to get caught up after being out of town, so other than two very brief phone conversations, Thea and I hadn't spoken since before I left on my trip."

"Did she say anything that would indicate she was worried about anything?" I asked.

"No. We spoke briefly on Monday of last week to set up the lunch on Saturday, and then for a minute when she called to cancel on Friday. She didn't say anything that would make me think she was in some sort of trouble."

"Gigi from the library said Thea asked her about county legal codes. Did she say anything to you about that?"

"No, never. I do know she temped at a law office a while back. I'm not sure which one, but I bet the temp agency she worked for would know."

"Thanks. I'll check with them."

Cody and I chatted with Kim for a few more minutes and then said our good-byes. We decided to stop off at the real estate office she'd referred to before going to the grocery store to pick up something to make for dinner and then heading home for our meeting with the entire sleuthing gang. We learned from the Realtor that Thea had been hired to answer phones and take messages, but it had been strictly a Monday-through-Friday thing; he hadn't asked her to do anything for him on Saturday. He did remember her mentioning she had a job on Saturday but would be available the following week if he needed her. I asked if she'd given any indication where that job was, but he hadn't asked and she hadn't said. We thanked him for his time and headed to the market.

Chapter 4

By the time Cody and I reached the market, the rain was coming down in sheets. He found a parking space as close to the door as he could and we made a mad dash from the truck to the store. News of the building storm must have made the rounds because most of the people we ran in to were stocking up on batteries, bottled water, and candles. Deciding we'd buy ingredients for a meal that could be made on my gas grill should the power go out, we settled on thick steaks, fresh salad, and crusty sourdough bread. For dessert, I chose brownies from the bakery.

We gathered everything we thought we'd need and got in line. While a stormy night didn't seem like a good time to hold a strategy session, everyone except Tara lived on Maggie's property. I'd called her earlier to tell her to bring her cat and an overnight bag and plan to stay with me rather than attempting to drive home. When she called back she said Parker Hamden, the doctor she'd been dating, had asked her to have dinner, so she'd have to miss the meeting. The repairs to the cat lounge had been completed and she was planning to be open the following day.

"I see you're stocking up just in case," Erica Jennings, one of my former history teachers, said as she got in line behind us.

"Better safe than sorry," I answered. "We're supposed to get quite a bit of rain and the peninsula road does tend to flood."

"As far as I'm concerned, this storm can move back out to sea. A little rain is a good thing, but this storm has already brought more than anyone needs."

"Cassie told me school was closed today."

Erica nodded. "And if there's flooding they'll close it tomorrow too. By the way, I ran into Finn at the gas station this morning and he told me that Thea Blane had died. I didn't know her well, but I did meet her once at the library. He was in a hurry, so I didn't have time to ask him about the details. Was it an accident?"

"I can't speak to the specific cause of death, but it appears foul play was involved. We'll know more once an autopsy is performed."

"It's such a shame. It seems our little island has suffered more than its share of violent deaths in the past couple of years."

"I don't disagree with you about that. I've been talking to some of Thea's friends and co-workers, but so far no strong motive has come to light."

"I'm not sure I should say anything, given the fact she's gone and therefore unable to defend herself, but one of the other teachers at the high school told me that Thea had been fired from one of her temp jobs for inappropriate conduct."

"Inappropriate conduct? What do you mean by that?"

"I understand she was caught going through files she hadn't been cleared to access. Please keep in mind I came across this information secondhand and have no direct knowledge of any wrongdoing on Thea's part, but it might be a good idea to check with the temp agency she worked for."

"I will. And thanks. At this point any lead is a worthwhile lead. They may not pan out, but I've found the more you dig, the more you find."

Cody and I didn't get home until it was after five. I went to see to the cats in the sanctuary while Cody took Max out for a quick walk. Siobhan saw us pull in and let us know she'd be over in a bit, though Finn was running late and wouldn't be joining us before six. The steaks wouldn't take long to grill, so I figured we'd put them on when he arrived.

******

By the time everyone arrived at the cabin the storm had intensified. Not only was the rain coming down at a rate of more than an inch an hour, but the wind had picked up, which caused the surf to pound the island from the west. It was warm and cozy in my cabin and we still had power, so I decided to enjoy my family and friends and not worry about what the storm was going to do.

Finn started off by telling us that he'd received a preliminary report from the medical examiner. He'd verified that Thea had died as a result of trauma to the head. It appeared as if she had been hit with a cylindrical object, but a search of the house hadn't resulted in any objects that matched the size and shape the ME had identified being found. Finn also said that lividity put the time of death at between two and five on Saturday afternoon.

I asked if he had spoken to Thea's neighbors. Only two of the five closest neighbors had been home on Saturday, and of the two, neither had noticed anything suspicious. Finn planned to interview the people who lived behind Thea the following day.

"How about you?" Finn asked me. "Have you uncovered anything that might be relevant?"

"Not really. Kim spoke to Thea on Friday, but only briefly. Thea told her that she had a job and needed to cancel their Saturday lunch date. So far no one I've spoken to seems to know who she planned to work for on Saturday. I think we need to contact the temp agency to get a list of her assignments."

"I did that today," Siobhan spoke up. "Thea temped at the dentist's office where her friend Kim works two weeks ago. She had a job for a photographer over the weekend and then worked in a realty office this past week. According to her supervisor, she wasn't working this weekend, and other than the job with the photographer, she didn't normally take jobs on Saturday and Sunday."

"So, if she did have a job on Saturday it must have been something she got herself rather than going through the agency," I said. "I ran into Mrs. Jennings at the market just now. She'd heard from another teacher that Thea had been fired from one of her temp jobs when she got into files she hadn't been authorized to access. Did the person you spoke to at the temp agency mention that?"

"No," Siobhan said. "But I didn't ask about it either. I can call back tomorrow."

"Find out if Thea had a temp job at a law office recently. Gigi at the library told me that she had been looking for information pertaining to local statutes."

"Okay. I'll ask about that as well."

I glanced at Finn. "We need to take another look at her house. Maybe she left a note about where she planned to be on Saturday."

"The crime scene guys have been over the place. I'm sure they would have found a note if there was one."

"Maybe. But I've found in the past that they're so busy looking for blood, hair, and clothing fibers they miss clues that are a bit subtler."

Finn shrugged. "Okay, but it's raining pretty hard. We should go now, before the road floods."

It was at that point that Apollo jumped up and ran to the door. It appeared he was in favor of searching Thea's house again as well. We decided to take Cody's truck because it was four-wheel drive with a high road clearance in case of flooding. I let Siobhan sit in the front, where there was more room, and was sandwiched in the back between Finn and Danny, with Apollo on my lap. It was slow going making our way through the flooded streets, but eventually we arrived at our destination.

Finn had a key he'd had the locksmith make, and we all followed him inside. As he'd indicated, it appeared the crime scene guys had gone through things. I set Apollo on the floor and watched to see what he would do while Danny and Cody headed upstairs and Finn and Siobhan went into the kitchen.

"Okay, kitty. Time to do your thing. What do you want us to find?"

Apollo trotted over to a small desk against the wall near the stairs, where the hallway separated the den and the main living area. There was a potted plant on top of the desk, and cubbies at the back of the writing surface, packed with paperwork. To the left of the writing area, in front of a cubbyhole filled with envelopes was a small calendar. On the page with last Saturday's date it said *Coffee Café at nine*. I wondered who Thea was meeting. Maybe someone from the coffee bar would remember who she was with.

I pulled the envelopes out of the first of the cubbyholes. It looked like Thea had filed recent bills there for easy access. I found a bill from the power company as well as one from the refuse company. There was an envelope from the bank and one from a credit card company. None seemed to be related to her death, so I replaced them and pulled out the envelopes in the middle cubby. The envelopes there looked like personal correspondence: cards she received for her recent birthday and several letters from friends. I felt strange reading her private mail, so I replaced them as well.

The third storage space—the one that had been behind the calendar—held a small notebook. Inside was a list of what looked to be initials followed by dates. I wasn't sure if these were important, so I decided to show it to Finn. The only other thing in that cubby was a coupon for two-for-one drinks at Shots on Thursday evenings.

I opened the center desk drawer and began rummaging around. There was an assortment of pens and pencils, sticky notes, and paper clips. Apollo was sitting on the floor next to me, seemingly content, so I had to think whatever I was supposed to find would be exactly where I was looking. In addition to the shallow center drawer were two deeper ones to one side. The top of the two held file folders that I quickly thumbed through. I didn't find anything of interest, though Thea's laptop was in the bottom drawer. I was about to try to log on to it when a loud crack of thunder shook the small house. Finn and Siobhan joined me from the kitchen.

"I think we should get back before the road floods and we can't," Siobhan said.

I looked toward the stairs. "I'll let Cody and Danny know."

"We're right behind you," Cody said as he came down the stairs with a box in his arms.

"What do you have?" I asked.

"Danny found a box of photos. I don't know if they're important or will lead to any clues, but I figured we could bring them with us and take a closer look at the cabin."

The trip back to the peninsula was a tense one as rain drenched the landscape and lightning lit up the sky. By the time we made it back I'd pretty much decided it had been foolish for us to have gone out into the storm in the first place. Max was anxiously awaiting our return, which made me feel bad we'd left him behind, although there really hadn't been any room for him in the truck.

Cody tossed a log on the fire, I made coffee, and Finn got Siobhan settled on the sofa with one of Aunt Maggie's homemade quilts. It did my heart good to see the way he doted on her even more than usual while she was pregnant.

"One thing's for sure," Danny said as he began thumbing through the photos. "Thea took a lot of pictures."

I sat down next to him as he sorted through them. Some of the photos were recent, some were old. It seemed there were photos of almost everywhere on the island. "It looks like some of these were taken in the hollow," I said.

"Do you think that's relevant?" Siobhan asked.

"I'm not sure. On one hand Thea has photos of the entire island, so having photos of the hollow isn't odd. However, Apollo is the one who led me to Thea's body, and he did first appear to me at the entrance to the hollow. It makes me want to find a link between the two. I suppose it's possible there is a link, but it's probably more likely there isn't."

"Some of these photos are pretty old," Danny pointed out. "This one was taken before the new wing was added onto the church."

"Look how young Father Kilian is," I said after Danny handed me a photo that showed him standing in front of the church with a young woman I didn't recognize.

"I doubt we'll find any clues among the photos unless we know what we're looking for," I concluded. "Although I guess the photos taken from the hollow do tell us Thea was most likely there at some point. Some of these photos look like they were taken recently."

"Do you recognize this man?" Danny asked, handing me a photo of a man who looked to be in his mid to late twenties. He wore a fishing vest and a floppy hat and was staring at something off in the distance.

"He doesn't look familiar. Why? Do you know him?"

"I don't think so, but he looks familiar. I guess I might have seen him around town. Maybe at O'Malley's."

"That's a good bet because you spend a lot of your time drinking and playing pool there," I teased.

"I'm bored. It'll be better when the whales return and I'm back to eighteen-hour days."

"Isn't this Thea with her ex?" Siobhan asked, passing me a photo of Thea and Steve Blane at the park during what looked to be a community picnic.

"It is. And they look so happy." Both were smiling at something that must have been beyond the view of the camera. Steve had his hand on Thea's shoulder and she had her head tilted toward his. "I'm pretty sure this was taken last summer. I can just make out the faces of the people in the background and I'm sure this one here," I pointed to the photo, "is Father Bartholomew."

"If Lilly was jealous of the fact that Steve was friends with his ex she may have had reason to be," Siobhan said after I passed back the photo. "Although there's nothing in the photo to suggest Thea and Steve had been hooking up romantically, the photo does have an intimate feel to it." Siobhan looked at me. "Did you ever have the chance to talk to Lilly?"

"No, not yet. But I see what you mean about the photo. I'll make a point of speaking to her tomorrow." I looked at the photo again. I knew Lilly and Steve were engaged, but the photo of Steve and Thea seemed to have captured an intimacy you wouldn't think would exist between two people who had been divorced for a decade. I wondered if we'd just stumbled onto our motive.

Chapter 5

Wednesday, March 14

After we'd looked through the photos last night we'd tried to access Thea's computer, but it was password protected. Cody said he'd work on getting into it and Finn took the photos. By the time we broke for the night we were all exhausted. Cody helped me with the cats in the sanctuary and then we settled in with Max and Apollo, while Finn, Siobhan, and Danny went to the main house. When I woke up in the morning the storm had passed.

Luckily, I didn't have to be at work until ten during the winter, which gave me plenty of time to take Max for a quick run. Living on the beach and being able to run along the water's edge was renewing and inspiring on any day, but the day after a storm, when everything was fresh and damp, was one of my favorite times. Today's jaunt would need to be a short one, so I took a deep breath and relaxed as I settled into a pace that allowed me to meditate on my day as I enjoyed the beauty around me.

The residents of Madrona Island generally enjoyed a slower pace in the winter. The ferry only stopped here twice each day; during the busy summer months it docked five times during the weekdays, six times on Saturday and Sunday. Given that a large percentage of the bookstore's sales came from visitors as they debarked the ferry, Tara and I enjoyed a slower pace as well.

I was at the point in my run when I was preparing to turn around and head back to the cabin to get ready for work, when Max trotted up to me with something in his mouth. "What do you have?" I asked my wet, sandy dog.

Max dropped the object, which turned out to be a man's black leather wallet, at my feet. I picked it up and opened it to find a wad of cash, several credit cards, a frozen yogurt punch card, a University of Washington ID card, and a driver's license that belonged to Travis Long. The wallet was completely soaked and the yogurt punch card had all but disintegrated, but I figured Travis would want his driver's license and credit cards back, so I took the wallet with me.

Back at the cabin, I fed Max and Apollo and then went upstairs to take a shower and get ready for work. I dressed in a pair of jeans and a pink Coffee Cat Books T-shirt before pulling on some tennis shoes and grabbing my Coffee Cat Books sweatshirt. I wouldn't have time for breakfast if I didn't want to be late, so I went directly to the cat sanctuary to feed everyone there and then load up the four cats I was bringing with me that day, figuring I'd grab a coffee and a muffin when I got to the store.

When the cats were loaded in the car I went back to the cabin to grab Travis Long's wallet and my backpack, which I used as a purse. As I opened the door, Apollo squeezed out and made a mad dash for the car. The doors were all closed, so he jumped up onto the hood and waited.

"I don't like to take my visiting cats to work," I explained to him. "That increases the risk that someone will see you and want to adopt you."

"Meow."

"I get that you don't want to stay home all day, but I think it's for the best." I leaned over to pick him up, but he bared his claws and hissed at me. "Okay, I give in; you can come. But you need to behave. Okay?"

"Meow."

I looked down at Max, feeling bad taking Apollo but leaving him behind again. "Maybe you can hang with Cody today." A quick call confirmed he was fine with the idea, so I opened the front passenger side door and let Max and Apollo hop in because the entire backseat was already taken up with the travel carriers filled with the four sanctuary cats. I decided it would be best to drop the cats off first, then take Max to the newspaper office, so I headed to Coffee Cat Books.

"Oh good, you're on time," Tara greeted me when I walked through the front door with the first of the four cats to be featured that day.

"Aren't I usually?" I asked as I removed the cat from the carrier and headed toward the cat lounge.

"We both know you're late more often than you're on time, but tardiness is part of your charm. Today, I need you to run to the printer to pick up the flyers for the annual spring sale. I just got a call that they're ready."

"I'll get the cats settled; then I need to drop Max off at the newspaper, but I'll go to the printer after that." I returned to the car for the next cat. Tara followed me out and grabbed another carrier. "You don't happen to know someone named Travis Long, do you?"

"No," Tara answered. "Why do you ask?"

"I found his wallet this morning. Well, Max found it. It must have washed up on the beach during the storm last night."

"Did it look as if it had been in the water long?"

"No," I answered. "Everything was waterlogged but mostly intact, so it probably had only been there for a day or less. I'll drop it off at Finn's office when I take Max to the newspaper. If I lost my wallet I'd check with the sheriff's office to see if anyone turned it in."

"That's a good idea. If Finn is in and you have the chance to speak to him, let him know I spoke with Victoria Grace this morning. She was visiting her sister in Portland all last week, so it looks like we can take her off the suspect list."

"Okay, I will. You should call Siobhan; she planned to speak to her today."

I got all four cats settled; then Max, Apollo, and I headed to the newspaper office. As we pulled up out front, I could see Cody working at the counter through the large picture windows along the entire front of the building. Max loved hanging out with

Cody, so he hopped out of the car and was headed to the front door before I had a chance to grab Apollo.

"Wait," I yelled at the independent cat. "It's too dangerous for you to be wandering out here by yourself."

The cat ignored me and took off trotting on the sidewalk. I quickly let Max into the reception area where Cody was working and then ran down the street, trying to catch up with Apollo. I should have put him in a cat carrier, but there hadn't been room on the front seat for both that and Max and me, so I'd let him ride beside us unrestrained.

"Apollo," I called as I picked up the pace. "Wait for me. You shouldn't be running around on your own. I'd hate for something to happen to you."

When Apollo arrived at the corner I held my breath, afraid he would run into the street. Instead, he made the turn onto Main and headed back toward the wharf and Coffee Cat Books. I thought the bookstore was his destination, but he stopped and waited for me to catch up when he arrived at Herbalities, Tansy and Bella's shop.

"You want to see Tansy?" I asked.

"Meow."

I opened the front door and Apollo darted inside. Bella was dusting shelves, but I didn't see Tansy.

"Good morning, Cait," Bella greeted me with a smile. "This must be Apollo."

"It is. It seems he wants to see Tansy. Is she here?"

"I'm afraid she's ill. She didn't come in today."

"Ill? Do you know what's wrong?"

Bella's smile faded. There was concern in her bright blue eyes. "I'm not sure. When she came home from the hollow on Monday she looked pale and worn out. I asked what was wrong, but she just said her energy was off and went straight to bed. When I checked on her yesterday morning she said she was feeling worse, so I suggested she stay in. She was still sleeping when I left today, but I'd already assured her I could handle things in the shop on my own."

"I'm so sorry she's feeling under the weather. Please tell her that I hope she feels better soon."

Bella bent down to pick up Apollo, who had wandered over to her.

"I don't suppose Tansy has had any further thoughts about what's going on in the hollow?" I asked.

Bella hugged the cat to her chest. "Not that she's said. I did have a vision last night, but I'm not certain it had anything to do with the disturbance in the hollow. Normally, everything cat related is Tansy's forte."

"What was your vision?" I asked.

"Tansy was standing on the beach, looking out toward the sea. I was looking at her from a distance, but I could feel her fear. I wanted to approach, but for some reason all I could do was observe. After a short time, an owl appeared from out of nowhere and landed on her shoulder."

"Do you think that means something?" I wondered.

"The presence of an owl can have many meanings. Generally, owl energy has been associated with intuition and the ability to see what others can't."

"That sounds like Tansy."

"Yes, it does. And that may be all my vison of the owl represented. But owl energy can also signal change, and the traditional meaning of the arrival of an owl is death."

"Okay, that's sounding less positive. Should we be doing something?"

Bella held the cat out and looked it in the eye. "I think Tansy's energy is tied to the hollow. If we can fix the imbalance there Tansy will be fine as well."

"It seemed the imbalance Tansy sensed was the tainted water. What if we can't fix the problem and the cats don't return?"

Bella bowed her head. "We can't allow that to happen."

I watched as Apollo jumped down and walked to the door. It seemed he was ready to leave. "We'll figure this out. Tell Tansy not to worry."

Apollo and I walked back toward Finn's office, which was next door to the newspaper. I wanted to give him the wallet I'd found, and it couldn't hurt to check in with him to see if he'd had any news regarding Thea's death since last night. If Tansy was sick because of the imbalance in the hollow I needed to solve Thea's murder quickly so I could work on that. I was beginning to wonder where my energy should be focused. Initially, I'd assumed finding Thea's killer was the priority, but now I wasn't certain.

I stopped at my car to put Apollo inside before grabbing the wallet from my change tray. I wouldn't be long, and the last thing I wanted to do was give Apollo the opportunity to take off again.

Finn was on the phone when I arrived, so I took a seat in the reception area and waited. He joined me there a few minutes later.

"Am I to assume you have information regarding Thea's death?" he asked.

"Not since last night," I said. "Tara found out Victoria Grace was out of town last week, so we can take her off the list. This is the reason I'm here." I handed Finn the wallet.

He opened it and looked at the ID. "Travis Long."

"Do you know him?" I asked.

"Mr. Long's girlfriend reported him missing yesterday. He's a student at the University of Washington and came to the island to do some research. He had a date with the girlfriend on Saturday night, but he never showed."

I frowned. "I suppose the fact that Max found his wallet on the beach isn't a good sign."

Finn pursed his lips. "No, I don't suppose it is. I'll follow up with the girlfriend to see if she's heard from him since we spoke. If she hasn't we'll need to consider the possibility that foul play is involved in his disappearance."

"I'm starting to get a bad feeling about things. First Tansy senses a disturbance in the hollow and we find out the cats have been leaving. Then we go to check it out and find the water has been tainted. The next thing we know, Thea's dead. To top it all off, I just found out Tansy is sick and Bella had a vison of an owl, and now the man whose wallet Max found is missing. What on earth is going on?"

"A vision of an owl?"

"It's a spirit animal thing. Apparently, it can represent insight and enhanced vision, or it can represent a change or death."

"So, which is it?"

"Bella didn't know. At this point all I can say for sure is that something bad is going on and it's up to us to identify and fix it."

Chapter 6

Apollo and I returned to Coffee Cat Books just as the first ferry of the day was about to dock, so I knew Tara and I would be busy until the crowd thinned out. Working in a location where most of our business came from passengers coming and going on the ferry, it seemed our work flow was feast followed by famine until the next ferry arrived and we did it all over again.

"Did you remember the flyers?" Tara asked.

I cringed. "I'm going right now. Can you keep an eye on Apollo for me?"

"I'll just put him in the cat lounge with the others for now. If anyone asks about him, I'll let them know he isn't available."

I left Coffee Cat Books for the second time that morning and headed to the printers. Tara had come up with the idea of running a huge sale at the bookstore each spring to clear out the old inventory and make way for the new, which we hoped to sell over the busy summer months. The sale had become a popular event, bringing visitors from the larger cities across the channel, which gave a boost to our bottom line.

The printer was in Harthaven, about a ten-minute drive from Pelican Bay. Harthaven was established by Madrona Island's founding fathers to serve the community that had developed when the island was first settled and was home to businesses that supported the local population to this day. Pelican Bay, on the other hand, was a new development that was born from the tourism that resulted from the ferry stopping on the island daily.

"Morning, Diane," I greeted the woman who owned Harthaven Printing. "I'm picking up the flyers Tara ordered."

"I have them right here. I can't wait for the sale. Last year I bought enough books to last the entire summer."

"I expect this year's sale to be just as awesome, but you should plan to come early. It seems we sold out most of the stock Tara had tagged for the sale within the first couple of days."

Diane handed me the order form to sign, indicating I had received the order.

"Is Coffee Cat Books planning to sponsor a booth at the Easter fair this year?"

"I'm sure Tara is, but I'll verify it and let you know for sure."

"It's on Saturday, March 31, and there are only two spots left, so have her call me this morning. We had a slow start getting folks to commit, but now that it's getting closer people have been bringing in their deposit checks at a steady pace."

"Hang on and I'll call Tara." I dialed my partner, who confirmed that she did plan to reserve a booth. I asked Diane to save us a spot and I'd be back with a check later that morning. I was about to leave with the flyers when Jared Pitman walked in. I remembered Pam had said she'd seen Jared with Thea at O'Malley's, so I waited while he picked up a box of envelopes and followed him out.

"I guess you heard about Thea," I began as we walked down the sidewalk toward the parking lot.

He nodded. "I'm sorry about what happened, but I'm not surprised. I tried to warn her, but she wouldn't listen."

"Warn her about what?"

Jared paused as he reached his car. He opened the back door and set the box on the seat. "Thea had been working on some sort of secret project. She told me that she'd stumbled onto some information a couple of months ago and insisted she knew things that could get some influential people into a lot of trouble. I told her it was best to forget what she knew and mind her own business, but she kept saying knowledge was currency and she was going to cash in."

"She was going to blackmail someone?"

"That was my take, although she never told me exactly what sort of information she had or who she planned to blackmail with it. I don't know for certain that her cockamamy plan was behind her death, but I won't be surprised if that's how it turns out."

"Did you tell Finn that?"

"Yes, I did. He said he'd look in to it."

"And you don't know anything else? Where she stumbled onto this information, what it pertained to, or who if anyone else she'd already shared the information with?"

Jared shook his head. "Thea refused to say anything else. We had some fun together, usually met for two-for-one Thursdays at Shots, but we didn't have the sort of relationship that led to the sharing of intimate secrets. We were just bar buddies. I'm not sure she would have told me anything at all if she hadn't been drunk at the time."

"Okay, well, thanks, and if you think of anything else call me or Finn."

"I will. I hope you catch the coward who hit her when she wasn't looking."

Jared got into his car and drove away, and I continued to my car and drove back to the bookstore. I gave the flyers to Tara and she sent me back to the printer's with our check. It was a beautiful sunny day, but the island was still recovering from the storm; schools had remained closed for one more day and Cassie had come in to help Tara and make some extra cash. When I brought the check to Diane she was standing at the counter chatting with Pam Wilkins.

"Oh good," Diane said. "Pam is here to drop off a check for Shells and Sunshine, so the booths for the Easter fair are officially sold out. When I agreed to take charge of registration, I had no idea how much time it would require."

"I think that's true of volunteer endeavors in general," Pam commented. She turned to me. "Do you have any news regarding Thea's death?"

"Not really. I've spoken to some people, and Finn's been looking into things, but neither of us has stumbled across anything conclusive. Thea was killed in her home and we didn't notice any sign of forced entry, so it appears she may have known her killer. Finn is waiting for a report from the crime lab. If he's lucky they'll come up with fingerprints or some form of physical evidence to point us in a direction."

"Have you spoken to Lilly Kent?" Pam asked.

"Not yet, but she's on my list. Do you know something about her?"

"It's not so much that I know something, but after we spoke yesterday I sat down and tried to make a list of who I thought would have had a strong enough motive to kill Thea and Lilly popped into my head. After Thea and I had our falling out Lilly asked me out for lunch. I guess she felt she'd find a sympathetic ear in me after what Thea had done. She told me that while she was in love with Steve and wanted to marry him, she was hesitant because of the tie he still had with Thea. I pointed out that even though they weren't married anymore their divorce seemed to have been amicable and they'd remained friends, but Lilly insisted that because they didn't have children together, they had no reason to communicate with each other on a regular basis, yet Thea still called Steve at least a couple of times a week, asking for help with one thing or another."

"Did Lilly say whether she'd spoken to Steve about the situation?" I wondered.

"She said she had, but he told her that Thea wasn't the handy sort and needed help with things around the house. I'm not saying Lilly would actually have killed Thea to get her out of the picture, but I'm betting she's pretty happy now that she no longer has to compete for attention from her own fiancé."

"I guess I can see that. I'll mention this to Finn, and if he hasn't already spoken to her, I'll see if I can track her down."

"Please don't tell her that I told you what I have. I don't need her angry with me. She seems like she might play dirty, if you know what I mean."

I was about to agree that Lilly did appear to have a temper when Diane jumped in. "Lilly told me that Thea was fired from her temp job with Caldwell and Benson."

"Caldwell and Benson the attorneys?" I clarified.

Diane nodded her head.

"I did hear that Thea had been fired from one of her temp jobs for inappropriate conduct, but I wasn't aware it was Caldwell and Benson," I commented.

"Keep in mind, my source is the local gossip network, which isn't always reliable, but you might want to talk to some of the employees at the law firm. They might have more insight regarding what really happened."

"Thanks. I will."

I left the printers and went directly to Finn's office. I didn't want to take time out of my day to reinterview the same people he'd already spoken to, but it was sounding more and more as if Lilly might have the strongest motive for wanting Thea out of the way. Of course, the blackmail tip Jared had provided was pretty juicy too. When I arrived at Finn's door it was locked, the sign he put on the door letting people know he was in the field and to call him if they had an emergency in place. I didn't think what I had constituted an emergency, so I headed next door to say hi to Cody only to find he was out and about as well.

I decided to check in with Tara; if she didn't need me perhaps I'd see if Siobhan wanted to have lunch. As the mayor of Madrona Island, she had access to a lot of information that wasn't public knowledge. Maybe she'd have some insight into the workings of Caldwell and Benson that would be useful should I decide to interview the employees.

"Drake Benson and Rupert Caldwell are snakes who've made a fortune taking on cases other attorneys didn't want to handle," Siobhan said as we walked down the street to a nearby diner to order salads.

"What do you mean?" I asked.

"They have a reputation for representing corrupt businesses that are attempting to skirt the law, or defendants who are obviously guilty. In other words, they make a living making sure the bad guy wins."

"I don't think I've ever met either man, although I've seen advertisements for the local office."

"The main office is in Seattle, but they operate several satellites, including the one in Harthaven. While Caldwell works with large businesses, Benson specializes in criminal law. Neither spends a lot of time on the island, but they show up occasionally. If Thea had a temp job at the local office, she was probably working for Bruce Wong. He's actually a decent guy who handles most of the cases on Madrona Island."

I took a sip of my ice tea before I spoke. "I heard Thea had been snooping around at one of her temp jobs, which resulted in her being fired. Also that she had uncovered something damaging she planned to use to blackmail someone. If Caldwell and Benson are known for taking on clients from the seedy side of humanity, maybe she really had something that got her killed."

"Perhaps."

"Do you think someone from Caldwell and Benson could have silenced her to protect their client?" I asked.

Siobhan shifted in her seat, pausing to rub her stomach. "I wouldn't be at all surprised if that was the case. Of course, I doubt either Benson or Caldwell would have done it themselves; I'm sure they have plenty of clients who would have been happy to take care of things on their behalf. Having said that, all we have now is a theory, and a theory absent proof is pretty much useless. I think we should see if we can find any evidence that Thea actually had damaging information and tried to use it as part of a blackmail scheme."

"I wonder if Finn pulled Thea's phone and banking records."

"I'm sure he has," Siobhan answered. "We can ask him. If he has them and hasn't mentioned anything, there's probably nothing there."

After lunch I went to the Coffee Café in Harthaven. According to Thea's desk calendar, she had been there at nine o'clock on the day she died. I hoped there would be an employee or two who remembered seeing her. If I was especially lucky I'd find someone who remembered who she was with.

Coffee Café was a cozy place that served breakfast and lunch as well as the coffee drinks they were named for. The owner had recently had a baby and was taking some time off, so I planned to speak to her assistant, Ana. I didn't know her well because she'd lived on the island for less than a year, but we'd chatted often enough that she recognized me when I came in.

"So, what has you slumming in this part of town?" Ana teased.

"I was in the area and wanted to chat with you for a minute. Can you take a quick break?"

"Yeah, I can arrange that." Ana poked her head into the kitchen and let whoever was on the other side of the door know she was going to step out for a few minutes. "What's up?" Ana asked when we sat down on one of the benches provided for outdoor diners.

"Do you know a woman named Thea Blane?"

"No, I don't think I do."

"She lived nearby and did temp jobs on the island. I'm afraid she passed away over the weekend, and I'm following up on a few details. According to her desk calendar, she planned to be here at nine o'clock on Saturday morning. I was hoping you or one of your staff had seen her and noticed who she was with."

Ana frowned. "I was here on Saturday. Can you describe her?"

"She had dark hair that fell to just below her shoulders. She was around forty years old and most people would describe her as quite beautiful." I tried to remember what she was wearing when I found her body. "She may have been wearing blue jeans and a yellow sweatshirt."

"I do remember her. She met a man I'd say was around thirty. Dark hair and good-looking. I heard her say she needed to stop by her house to pick up something she'd forgotten, so they took their coffee to go."

"Can you remember anything else?"

"Not really. It was busy, and they weren't here long."

"Do you remember seeing either of them in the café before?"

"The woman no, but the man has been in on several occasions over the past month or so. He normally comes in earlier, though, like around six. He always gets a large coffee to go."

"Has he ever given you his name?"

Ana shook her head. "Not that I recall. Sorry. I wish I could be of more help."

Chapter 7

Most Wednesday nights you can find Cody and me at St. Patrick's, holding practice for the children's choir. This week was no different. I hadn't been sure I wanted to take on the role of choir director when I first was approached about it, but I'd come to find I quite enjoyed working with the kids.

"Cody's going to pass around the lyrics to the song we want to introduce on Sunday," I announced. "We'll sing it first as a group and then we'll select individuals to perform the solos," I announced.

Most of the kids wanted a chance to do a solo, so Cody and I tried to rotate them so everyone had an opportunity to shine. Naturally, some of the kids had more talent than others, and it seemed there were often arguments about the solos being given to those with the most to offer, not necessarily to the choir member who was next in line.

Cody passed out the music and then asked the woman who'd volunteered to play the piano to run through the number a couple of times so the kids could get a feel for the melody. I tried to follow along but, despite my effort, I found I was distracted this evening by Thea Blane's murder. Danny had spoken to John Walkman, who'd admitted she had angered him to the point of wanting to cause her bodily harm but insisted he hadn't been the one to kill her. I couldn't quite decide if I believed him.

Danny said John had a problem controlling his emotions and had been kicked out of O'Malley's on a number of occasions for participating in bar fights when he'd had too much to drink. We discussed the likelihood that John had actually been the one to hit Thea over the head, and Danny and I both thought he should remain on the suspect list. Danny suggested we add another of Thea's male friends, Walter Bodine. According to my brother, Walter and Thea dated from time to time, though they weren't really considered an item. Danny thought Walter was a lot more serious about Thea than she appeared to be about him.

I offered a few suggestions after the kids had gone through the song for the second time. Cody asked them to run through the parts he'd chosen to be sung as solos, while I allowed my attention to drift back to the murder case. While we'd identified several people who seemed to have motives, I didn't feel I had a strong suspect. Lilly Kent and John Walkman had worked their way to the top of my list, yet the idea that Thea may have come across information she planned to use to blackmail someone intrigued me the most. The next thing to do would be to try to find out what that information was, and who was most likely to be injured if it became public knowledge. The combination of Thea having worked for and been fired by Caldwell and Benson and her asking Gigi about county legal information led me to believe she might very well have known something worth killing for.

"Miss Cait," Polly Pintner asked, drawing me from my musings.

"Yes, Polly? How can I help you?"

"Are we going to do a special performance for Easter Sunday like we did last year?"

"We are," I responded to the eight-year-old with long red hair and bright blue eyes. "The song Cody is teaching you tonight will be part of our Easter lineup."

"My grandma is coming all the way from Boston to spend Easter with us. My mom said she would buy me a new dress, but only if I had a special part. I don't like to sing alone 'cause it makes butterflies in my stomach, but maybe I can do something else. Last year we had those cards Bethany held up. If we're going to have the cards again maybe I can do that job."

"Cody and I haven't discussed whether we're going to use the picture cards again, but I'll talk to him tonight and let you know. If we don't use them maybe we can find something else for you to do where you can stand out without having to do a solo."

Polly seemed happy with my answer and trotted over to rejoin the others. Cody was almost done with the song they'd been rehearsing, and I realized he'd probably need the sheet music for another song we planned to use for Easter Sunday. I'd meant to make copies before choir began but had been distracted and had never gotten around to it. I grabbed my original and held it up in the air, letting Cody know I was heading down the hall to make the copies.

When I arrived in the small room that contained a printer, a computer terminal, and a copy machine, I found Father Bartholomew making copies, probably for his Bible study group.

"I'm just about finished," he said.

"That's fine. Take your time. Cody is with the kids. I really enjoyed your sermon last Sunday. I meant to stop by after Mass to tell you how much."

"Thank you. I thought it was well received. It's been a difficult transition for the members of the community to accept me in the role Father Kilian filled for so many years, but I feel I'm finally being accepted."

"You totally are. I've heard nothing but positive things since you joined us."

"How is Michael doing in his own transition?" Father Bartholomew asked me. He was one of the few people who knew that Father Kilian had chosen to leave the priesthood altogether after retiring to marry my Aunt Maggie.

"I think he's doing fine. Michael and Aunt Maggie have been spending a lot of time together, and they'll be heading toward the final step in their plan sooner rather than later. I know there'll be members of the congregation who won't understand or approve of their marrying, but they really deserve to have this time."

"I agree. And I wish them the best." Father Bartholomew removed his original from the copier. "I wanted to ask about Thea Blane, Caitlin. I tried calling Deputy Finnegan, but we seem to keep missing each other. I haven't been approached by anyone regarding a funeral. With Easter week just around the corner, I thought it would be best to plan it as soon as is possible."

"Thea was divorced and never had children. I don't know who her next of kin might be. I'm sure Finn has looked in to it, though. I'll ask him to call you when I see him later this evening. The fact that she was murdered might prevent a quick funeral even if next of kin is located."

"Do you have any news on that front?" Father Bartholomew asked.

"No, but there is something I'd like to ask you. I know you won't necessarily be able to answer, but I feel it could be important."

"I don't suppose it would hurt for you to ask."

"It's been suggested to me that Thea had been planning to blackmail someone. I don't suppose she mentioned anything to you that would suggest that information is correct?"

Father Bartholomew shook his head. "If you're wondering if she might have mentioned a blackmail scheme in confession, you're right, I wouldn't be able to tell you as much. But she never confessed anything along those lines. I did see her deeply involved in a conversation with one of our new parishioners after choir practice on Tuesday of last week."

"And who was that?"

"Paul Gibson."

I frowned. "Paul Gibson is an attorney."

"I believe he's retired now, but I do remember someone mentioning to me that he used to practice law."

"Do you have his phone number?"

"I don't, but I know he's friendly with your brother Aiden. Why don't you talk to him about contacting Paul?"

"I'll do that. Thanks."

I made my copies and went back to Cody and the kids. I gave everyone a copy of the sheet music and then Cody asked the pianist to run through the song several times. Cody seemed to have things under control, so I stepped out into the hallway and called my oldest brother.

"Hey, Cait," Aiden answered in his deep voice. "What's up?"

"Do you know someone named Paul Gibson?"

"He's in the group I play poker with on Fridays. Why do you ask?"

"I think he might have some information that will help me with the murder investigation I'm working on. I don't suppose you'd be willing to give me his phone number?"

"I'll call him and have him call you. Are you talking about the Thea Blane case?"

"I am. It seems Thea may have come across some sort of information when she was working at Caldwell and Benson that she intended to use to blackmail someone. I don't know the specifics, but I also know she had some legal questions, and Gigi from the library suggested she speak to Paul."

"You think Thea was killed because of a blackmail scheme?"

"I don't know for sure, but it seems like a possibility. Have you heard anything?"

Aiden hesitated before answering. "I might know something. I don't want you getting hurt, though, so I'm not sure I should tell you about it."

"I'm not a child and I won't get hurt. If you know something, you need to tell me. Tansy isn't feeling well. I need to get this murder case wrapped up so I can fix the problem in the hollow."

"What problem in the hollow and what's wrong with Tansy?"

I briefly explained about the tainted water and the disappearance of the cats. Aiden asked what any of that had to do with Tansy, and I admitted I didn't know, but it seemed her health was in some way connected to the health of the hollow.

"Okay," Aiden said. "I'll tell you what I know, but not over the phone. Are you at home?"

"Choir practice."

"If you and Cody want to stop by my place on your way home I'll show you what I have."

"We'll be there. Thanks, Aiden."

******

Aiden was a fisherman by trade, so he was away from home more often than not. He used to live with Mom and Cassie in our childhood home, but after it burned to the ground he decided to get his own space. Now he lived in a small house in Harthaven. As far as bachelor pads went, it wasn't bad, just a block from the marina where he kept his boat and within walking distance from a bar and a couple of restaurants.

He invited us in and offered us a beer, which we declined. There was a box sitting on the table that looked as if it contained files of some sort. I wasn't sure if these were the items he wanted to show us, or if he'd been doing his taxes when I called.

"Before I tell you what I know I need you both to promise you'll be cautious in deciding what to do with this information," he started off.

"Of course. What is it?" I asked, impatient to get on with it.

"A buddy of mine who runs a fishing charter told me that he'd been looking to buy a house with a deep-water dock so he could move out of the marina. There aren't a lot of places like that on the south shore, but there are several on the north shore, so that's where he's been looking. Anyway, he said he met with a guy who told him that someone had put in an offer to buy the old Smith Packing building."

Smith Packing had been closed for over five years, but before it had gone under it was a large plant that employed a lot of people. The building was old and rundown, but it was on a large piece of land right on the water and could be valuable to the right person.

"What does that have to do with anything?" I asked.

"The building is tied up in a contingency, based on their ability to get a permit to thin trees in the forested areas of the island, by a group that wants to use the property for a sawmill. If the permit is granted the sale will be finalized; if it isn't the deal falls through."

"Thin trees? You mean cut them down? Aren't there regulations against that?"

"There are, but thinning is an accepted fire prevention practice, and this group has taken on similar projects in other areas. If you ask me, it seems likely they'll be successful in getting a permit to thin the forest along the old logging road on the north shore. The problem they're likely to run in to is with the trees in the hollow."

I frowned. "The hollow is a protected area."

"Traditionally it has been, but it's private land."

Nora Bradley owned that land. Her husband, our ex-mayor, had tried something similar to harvest the Madrona trees but had been killed before it could be executed. I couldn't believe the problem had resurfaced.

"Do you think Nora will allow the trees to be cut?"

"I don't know. But the trees in the hollow have been left to grow and multiply, making the density of the vegetation impassable. While it presents a very real risk in terms of fire, especially if the island were to suffer a long drought, it hasn't been logged mainly due to the cost of building a road and the cats that live there. The group that wants to log the area is willing to cover the cost of the road, which means the only real obstacle they're facing is—"

"The cats," I finished for him. "Do you think they would taint the water to drive the cats away?"

Aiden shrugged. "I have no idea what they'd be willing to do, but I found the timing of the tainted water interesting."

"What does this have to do with Thea?" Cody asked.

"The logging company is being represented by Caldwell and Benson. Paul mentioned to me that they'd fired Thea. Paul didn't make a connection between the logging project and Thea's dismissal, but after she died he remembered her asking him about the consequences of tampering with the environment for financial gain. Please keep in mind, this is only a theory, and neither Paul nor I have any proof whatsoever, but given the events of the past few days it seems reasonable Thea came across some information about the logging project while temping at Caldwell and Benson and realized it could be of value."

"So she tried to blackmail either the logging company or Caldwell and Benson and was killed for her efforts," I said.

"Like I said, it seems to be a possibility. I don't want you getting in the middle of this. I called Finn and told him everything I just told you. Let him do his job. If there's any truth to it he'll find the evidence he needs."

I didn't argue, but I didn't agree either.

"Promise me," Aiden said in his threatening, big-brother voice.

"Oh, all right. But I'm not going to stop investigating the murder just in case this goes nowhere."

I glanced at Cody, who looked at Aiden. I could tell he agreed with my brother that I should leave this to Finn, but he knew I wasn't likely to do that. That was one of the things I loved most about Cody. He let me be me, even when he worried that being me wasn't necessarily the best thing for me.

Chapter 8

Thursday, March 15

Cody called to set up an appointment to speak to someone in the group that wanted to log the hollow on behalf of the newspaper. Neither of us had a clue as to whether an interview would result in any information we didn't already have, but it was a place to start. I'd talked to Finn about the blackmail theory and he said he'd been through Thea's financial records and hadn't found any indication she'd come into money from any source. Of course, that didn't mean she hadn't tried to blackmail someone and failed.

I woke up late on Thursday morning and got a late start. The cats needed to be tended to and Max needed a walk. By the time I arrived at Coffee Cat Books the first ferry had docked and the store was packed. I tied a Coffee Cat Books apron around my waist and took my spot behind the counter at the coffee bar.

"What can I get you?" I asked a petite blonde with deep blue eyes who was dressed in a khaki outfit that looked like she was about to set off on a safari.

"A soy latte with a single pump of vanilla."

I grabbed a cup and began to assemble the drink. "Is this your first time on Madrona Island?" I asked while I waited for the milk to steam.

"Yes. I only moved to the West Coast this past fall. I was born and raised on the East Coast, but I decided to spread my wings a bit and go to college out here at the University of Washington."

I handed the girl her cup and accepted a twenty-dollar bill. "So how are you liking it?" I asked as I made change.

"So far, a lot. I've made some good friends and the school has an excellent environmental sciences department. I'm just in my first year and I've already been assigned to work part time with a grad student on a research project."

"The grad student wouldn't be Travis Long, would it?"

She appeared surprised by my question. "Yes, I am working with Travis. How did you know?"

I looked around the crowded room. "I don't suppose you could wait for a few minutes? I want to talk to you about Travis, but I should finish with the customers in line before I take a break."

She looked uncertain.

"You can wait for me in the cat lounge, over there." I pointed. "I shouldn't be long."

"Okay, if you think it's important. Maybe I'll take one of those lemon muffins too."

"Thank you. I'm Cait."

"Beth."

I handed her the muffin. "I'm happy to meet you, Beth. The muffin is on the house and I won't be long, I promise."

Once the crowd had mostly cleared out I filled Tara in on what was going on and went into the cat lounge to talk with Beth, who was holding Apollo and talking to the other cats.

"Thank you for waiting," I began.

"Is Travis okay? I have to admit you have me worried."

"I'm not sure how Travis is. All I know is that I found his wallet on the beach and his girlfriend has reported him missing."

Beth frowned. "Girlfriend? Travis doesn't have a girlfriend."

"I don't know the name of the woman who called the sheriff's office. I found a wallet on the beach with his ID and credit cards inside and turned it in to the resident deputy. That was when I was told his girlfriend had reported him missing. I didn't ask any questions beyond that."

Beth set Apollo on the floor and looked at me. "I don't know who called, but I know Travis doesn't have a girlfriend."

"Perhaps Finn was mistaken. Would you mind if I asked what you're working on?"

"Travis's project deals with water quality. He's looking for natural and inexpensive ways to improve it on a global level, and as part of it he's testing water in various elevations, climates, and population densities. He's attempting to evaluate both naturally occurring and human-driven cultural and environmental changes that can impact the clarity of water."

"Can you give me an example?"

"There are quite a few things in the environment that have long been known to impact water quality: the use of insecticides, manipulation of naturally occurring drainage systems when developing raw land, climate change, and, of course, human-caused pollution. Travis hoped to find a way to counteract some of the negative changes to water quality by means other than adding chemicals to the mix. It's his opinion that before a fix for poor water can be implemented it's important to understand the factors that impact water quality on a chemical level."

"When was the last time you spoke to him?"

"It must have been Thursday of last week. He called me from his cell phone, but the reception was bad, so he said he'd email me a list of the items he needed. I received the list later that night."

"So, as far as you know, Travis didn't plan to return home this past weekend."

"He initially planned to, but he ran into some interesting data and wanted to stay on another week or two. He needed the items he asked me to bring so he wouldn't have to go back to restock his supplies."

"Where and when had you arranged to meet him?" I asked.

"I couldn't get away until today, so I told him I'd bring the things he asked for to the motel where he's staying."

"And which motel is that?"

"The Madrona Motor Inn."

"I know where that is. It's sort of a dive, but it's off the beaten path and less expensive than the other lodging properties on the island. Would you mind terribly if I went along with you to check it out?"

Beth frowned. "What exactly is going on? You said you found Travis's wallet, but you gave it to the resident deputy. Why do you want to come with me to meet Travis?"

I supposed if I wanted this woman's help I needed to be honest with her. "I don't want to worry you, but there've been some odd things going on over the last couple of days and it's possible Travis might know something about them."

"Such as?"

"First, the location where I'm willing to bet Travis took his water samples is locally known as the hollow. A large percentage of the island's feral cats live there, but many of them have left recently. My friend and I went to the hollow on Monday to try to find out what was going on with the cats and discovered the water was tainted. I don't know for certain that the water we examined is the same one Travis has been testing. I'm suggesting that we see if he's at the motel. You can follow my car; I know exactly where the motel is."

She agreed, and I told Tara where we were going before we headed north to the Madrona Motor Inn, which was on the coast road that encircled the island, to the north of Harthaven. It was a fifteen-minute drive, which gave me time to try to make sense of what was going on.

After leaving Pelican Bay and going north, the road hugged the coastline, providing a beautiful, serene drive. It was only March, so we still had a few weeks of cooler temperatures, but the sunny skies and gently rolling waves were a reminder that the long days of summer were just around the corner. The whales would start to migrate back to the area in May and tour operators like Danny would gear up for the busy tourist season, which impacted our small community in a major way. During the off season we enjoyed a laid-back, quiet way of life, but at the peak of the summer season the population almost doubled. Most years I was excited for the busy summer season to begin but just as anxious for it to end a few months later.

I slowed my vehicle as we came to the outskirts of Harthaven. The motel was farther north, but the only way to travel north of the small seaside town was to drive through it. There were times I was impatient with the twenty-mile-per-hour speed limit through the center of Harthaven, but today I was content to be out in the sunshine.

Once the incorporated area was behind me the speed limit rose to forty-five. I sped up slightly after navigating a sharp curve and headed toward the motel, which was just a few miles away. Upon arrival I pulled into the empty parking lot and waited for Beth to join me.

"Do you know which room Travis is in?" I asked when we got out of our cars.

"Room ten."

We walked over and knocked on the door. No answer. Beth looked at her watch, while I glanced around the property.

"Maybe he's out for the day," Beth suggested.

"Let's check with the desk clerk."

Beth nodded and followed me to the small office at the front of the building. I introduced myself to the young man working the desk and asked if he knew when Travis might be back.

"Haven't seen him for a few days," he answered.

"Did he mention that he was leaving the island?" I asked.

"Nope."

"Did he check out?"

"Nope."

"Is his stuff still there?" Beth asked.

"Far as I know. He paid for the room through the end of the month. I gave him the monthly rate, which doesn't include maid service. No one's had a reason to enter the room."

Beth glanced at me. I could see the concern in her eyes.

"Beth is a friend and colleague of Mr. Long. He asked her to bring him some supplies, which she has. I don't suppose you could open the door so we could drop off the things he wanted?"

The clerk looked at Beth, then back at me.

"Please?" Beth said. "Travis really needs this stuff."

"Okay," the clerk eventually answered. "I'll open the door, but just so you can drop the stuff off."

The clerk grabbed the key and Beth and I followed him to room ten. He opened the door and gasped. I looked over his shoulder and realized things had just become a lot more complicated.

Chapter 9

I called Finn, and Beth and I waited for him in my car. The room where Travis had been staying had been the scene of a violent attack. Not only were there items on the floor, which would suggest there'd been a struggle, but there was blood on the floor.

"Do you think whatever happened to Travis had anything to do with his research?" Beth asked.

"I would say it's a possibility."

Beth's face grew pale. "Do you think he's dead?"

I paused and then answered. "I don't know, but Finn might know more. We'll ask him when he gets here."

"Finn?"

"Deputy Ryan Finnegan. He's the resident deputy and my brother-in-law. He's a good guy. You can trust him."

Beth looked down at her entwined hands without responding. I understood her fear and anxiety. I was afraid of what Finn might tell us and I'd never even met the man, while Beth had been working closely with him for several months. I couldn't imagine what she must be feeling.

"What was Travis hoping to do with his research?" I asked, mostly to distract her.

"Travis is interested in clean water. He's been working on a filtration system that would remove toxins from water in naturally occurring rivers, lakes, and streams. It's a revolutionary idea that has had promising results in the lab but not yet in nature, so he's been testing groundwater in different areas to find water systems that are both isolated and contaminated."

I was about to ask Beth about the type of contaminants he was looking for when Finn's car pulled up. I introduced him to Beth and he asked her a few questions, many of them the same as my own. Then he told us to wait outside while he went into the room to look around. I wished I could assure Beth there was nothing to worry about, but the truth of the matter was, what I believed was the opposite.

A short while later, Finn emerged from the room. Beth and I waited for him to approach.

"So?" I asked.

"It appears an altercation of some type occurred in the room. I'm going to have the crime scene guys come over from San Juan Island to do a full workup. They'll be looking for fingerprints, DNA, whatever they can dig up. I saw there wasn't a computer in the room. I assume Long had one."

"He did," Beth confirmed. "There should also be vials with water samples, as well as chemicals to test the water."

"I didn't see anything like that." Finn looked around the empty parking lot. "It appears his car is gone as well. Do you know what he was driving?"

"Travis owns a black truck. Four-wheel drive. A Toyota, I think. An older model with a dent in the right front bumper."

"Do you happen to know the license plate number?" Finn asked.

Beth's eyes grew big. "Actually, I do. It's a Washington State vanity plate that says AQUAMAN."

"Aquaman? Is he in to comics?" Finn asked.

"He's in to water. Pure and clear water, to be specific. But yeah, he enjoys comics as well."

Finn jotted down a few notes. "Okay. That will do it for now. Are you staying on the island?"

"I planned to go back on the last ferry, but now I'm not sure," Beth answered. "I do have classes I shouldn't miss."

"I think it will be fine if you return to Seattle," Finn said. "I have your contact info if I have additional questions."

Beth looked at me. "Thank you for bringing me up here. Will you let me know what you find out?"

"I will. And take my cell number as well. Call me as often as you'd like."

"Thank you. I appreciate that." Beth looked toward her car. "What should I do with the supplies I brought for Travis?"

"You can leave them with me," I offered. "I'll see he gets them as soon as we catch up with him."

******

"Poor Beth," Tara said when I returned to Coffee Cat Books and explained what had happened.

"She's pretty worried about Travis. They'd been working together for months and became friends as well as colleagues."

Tara picked up a box she'd just emptied and set it aside. Then she opened the next box in the pile and began restocking the pink Coffee Cat Books mugs we sold. "How does this all fit together? First Tansy senses the cats are leaving the hollow, then you find Thea bludgeoned to death in her home, and now you discover a visiting scientist has disappeared."

"Beth said he'd been testing water over time. I can't help but feel he's somehow connected with whatever's going on in the hollow. I'm not sure how Thea fits into all of that, or if she even does, but I have a bad feeling about the whole thing."

"Do you think someone is intentionally tainting the water?" Tara asked.

"That's exactly what I think is happening. If I had to guess I'd say the group who want to log the hollow got hooked up with a couple of corrupt attorneys who advised them that they'd never get their permit as long as the cats were there. So, someone came up with the idea of tainting the water so the cats would leave. Thea found out when she was temping for the law firm and came up with the idea of cashing in on what she knew. She never got paid; instead, she was murdered for her effort. Meanwhile, Travis Long was here testing the water for his project and noticed the anomalies in the hollow. He investigated, and the bad guys found out and killed him. Max found his wallet on the beach. I'm betting his body was dumped in the sea."

"How can we prove or disprove your theory?" Tara asked.

I frowned. "I don't know."

She put another empty box aside and opened a third, this one filled with new releases. She began to organize the new books table as we continued our conversation, and I tried to pay attention to the conversation, but I found myself struggling to concentrate. I glanced out the front window and noticed our part-time employee, Willow Wood, walking across the parking area. "It looks like Willow is on her way in."

"Yeah. She called earlier and said she had a doctor's appointment and would stop by after. I miss her now that she isn't coming in every day."

"I've been missing her too." I smiled as Willow came in through the front door. "I'm so glad you stopped by. I've been wondering how you've been doing. How was your appointment?"

"Good. Everything is on track. The doctor thinks the baby may come sooner than initially predicated. In fact, he said there's a possibility he'll be here by this time next month."

"That's great. Are you ready?" I asked.

Willow rubbed her stomach with her right hand. "Yes and no. Alex has the nursery all set up and I'm excited to meet my baby, but I'm nervous too. Now that I've made the decision to keep the baby I find myself feeling overwhelmed. It such a big step, and at times I worry that I might not be up to taking on everything a parent is required to do."

"Well, I think you'll be a fantastic mother. And Alex seems excited about helping with the baby, so you won't be doing this parenting thing alone."

Willow smiled. "Alex has been great. I think he's more excited for the baby to get here than even I am. I just hope it's not all too much for him. Having a baby in the house will be challenging. The two of us are getting along so well, but we've only known each other for a few months. I'd be lying if I didn't say I'm worried about how a baby will change the dynamic we're still getting used to."

After everything that had gone on in December, I was fairly certain Alex was destined to help raise the exceptional child Willow carried. Of course, I couldn't simply tell her that one of my witchy friends had had a vision of a future in which her child would do great things, so I just told her to trust the relationship she was building with Alex would stand the test of time. Tara and I had discussed giving Willow a baby shower. If the baby was going to come early, it seemed prudent that we start planning the event soon.

"I'm surprised Alex isn't with you today," Tara said. "Hasn't he been going to all your doctor appointments with you?"

"He's visiting his father. I'm not sure if I mentioned it the last time I was here, but Balthazar has approached Alex about staying on Madrona Island permanently and running his business."

Balthazar Pottage was a very rich man who owned a variety of different enterprises that he managed from his own island.

"That's a wonderful idea," I said. "Alex hasn't really settled into anything since graduating from college. I realize with the money Balthazar has given him, he doesn't need to work, but everyone needs a purpose. Alex is a smart and very personable guy. I think with a little instruction from his father he'll do a wonderful job."

"I think so too. At first I think Alex was uncertain about it, but after he gave it some thought he realized it was the perfect solution for him and his father. He wants me and my baby to stay on the island with him, but I'm not sure about it."

"Alex is a good guy and he really seems to care about you," Tara said.

"He is a good guy. And I care about him too. But I don't know if I can ask him to help me raise another man's child."

"A lot of stepparents happily raise the child of their new spouse," I said gently.

"That's true, I guess. But right now, Alex and I are just friends. When he asked me to move in with him we agreed to keep it casual until after the baby was born. We have a lot of fun together, and I guess I can see myself eventually wanting to take the next step with him, but I don't want to do that for the wrong reason."

"Wrong reason?" Tara asked.

"Alex is a millionaire and I'm a homeless pregnant woman with no ties to anyone or anything. I would never want to get serious with Alex if there was any question in either of our minds that I was doing it to provide a secure future for my baby."

I put my hand on Willow's shoulder. "So don't rush it. Have the baby, but keep things the way they are for now. I suspect time will provide the answers you need."

Willow smiled. "Thanks. I appreciate that. And you're right. I have time to decide. Alex hasn't put any pressure on me to move things along at a pace

I'm not comfortable with." A softness came over Willow's face. "And he really is the best guy. Not only is he selflessly taking care of me during this tough time, but he's been thinking about his father as well. He even asked me how I felt about eventually moving Balthazar in with us. In his own wing, of course."

"Balthazar is an old man and I do worry about him living all alone on an isolated island, but I have a feeling convincing him to move won't be easy. Still, I agree with Alex; it does make sense. And if he doesn't feel comfortable being in the house where he lived with his wife, you can always build him a cottage nearby."

"That's something to consider." Willow grimaced as she shifted in her seat. "I should get going. Alex will be home soon. He'll worry if I'm not there."

"Did he take the ferry?" Tara asked.

"No, he took the boat. He said it was faster, and I guess it is. It was nice talking to you both. Maybe we can have lunch the next time I'm in town."

We both said we'd welcome the opportunity to catch up.

After Willow left Tara went over the cat adoption applications she'd taken that day with me. Both were from locals I knew well enough that an extensive background check wouldn't be necessary; I called the two women and asked them if they'd be willing to meet me at the cat sanctuary at five. They were, so I began loading the cats into the carriers.

"Are you planning to come by this evening?" I asked Tara as she helped me load the car.

"I am. I don't have anything else on my calendar this week."

"How are things with Parker? I'd hoped things were better when you said you had a date last night."

Tara had been dating Parker for over a year. Initially, they'd been serious about each other, but lately their relationship had stalled.

"Nothing's really wrong and we still enjoy each other's company, but it seems like our relationship has hit a wall. We went out to dinner last night, but it felt forced. There's nothing I can really put my finger on; nothing's really wrong, but nothing's right either. It might be that Parker's hesitant to move forward in our relationship because he's uncertain how it would affect Amy. To be honest, I've had the same concern myself."

"Amy seems to really like you."

"She does. And I like her, I don't think that's the problem. I think the problem is that Parker doesn't want to do anything that will rock the very fragile equilibrium he's been living with since Amy's mother went to prison. While Amy and I get along great, she's very dependent on Parker. The next logical step for us would be to move in together, but I don't think Parker's willing to risk it as long as Amy is so needy."

"Are you going to break up?" I asked as I carried another cat carrier out to the car.

"No. At least I don't plan to. I'm not sure what Parker's thinking. I'm all right continuing as we are, but I feel like Parker's pulling away. Before last night, he canceled two dates in a row, and when he dropped me off last night we didn't make any plans for the future. He says he's really busy right now, and maybe he is, but I think there's more going on than that. I guess I'll just have to wait and see how things work out. In the meantime, I have friends who mean the world to me to hang out with, and I'm grateful for that."

"And we're happy to have you. Danny said he'd bring a pizza tonight, so why don't you plan to come by at around six?"

"I'll be there. I'll even bring dessert."

******

When I arrived home, I found Melvina Lively, the first of the two women who'd filled out adoption paperwork, waiting for me. I asked her to give me a few minutes to settle the cats who weren't being picked up that evening. It occurred to me as we were chatting that Melvina was a member of the adult choir at St. Patrick's and would have known Thea. I offered her a seat in the office area of the sanctuary as soon as I was finished with the other cats.

"We know each other, so we can bypass many of the adoption formalities," I began. "I do want to go over the cat's health and shot records, as well as the guide we provide outlining the care of your new family member, beginning with acclimating him to his new home."

My standard spiel took about fifteen minutes. When I was done I brought up the subject of Thea and her untimely death.

"I heard about Thea just this morning," Melvina informed me. "I'm sorry about what happened, but I can't say I'm surprised."

"Why is that?"

Melvina moved in slightly and lowered her voice, even though we were the only two in the building.

"It's common knowledge Thea has struggled financially. The poor dear couldn't seem to hang on to a job, so she had to take on all the temporary jobs she could get."

"It did seem like she worked a lot," I agreed. "At least lately."

"When she was married her husband brought in enough money to support them; she began struggling after the divorce. Anyway, Thea's financial distress seemed to have intensified to the point where she felt she might lose her home. We discussed the matter on more than one occasion; then I ran into her at the market last week and she told me that her worries were a thing of the past. I asked her what had happened to turn things around and she told me she had a plan to boost her income. Something about the way she said it made me think she was in to something illegal."

"Why did you think that?"

"For one thing, the secrecy. She refused to provide any details. The whole thing was just so hush-hush. I had no idea why she brought it up at all if she wasn't going to tell me anything about it."

By the time I finished talking with Melvina the other woman had arrived. I went through my orientation one more time before sending her off with her new baby.

I quickly fed everyone and cleaned all the cat boxes before heading back to my cabin to take a quick shower and change into my clothes before my guests arrived.

Chapter 10

Madrona Island in the spring can be an interesting place. We'd had days of rain and cool temperatures, but this evening the temperature was almost balmy. The wind was nonexistent and the sky was a deep, clear blue, so I'd decided to set the table outside on the deck overlooking the ocean. Sunset wasn't until about seven-fifteen and we'd have thirty minutes of light after that, so my plan was to eat and relax for a bit before we went inside and launched into the latest information about the increasingly complicated investigation.

"I had an interesting call today," Danny started in after we had all served ourselves and had settled around my pine picnic table.

"Interesting how?" I asked after taking a bite of the cheese slice I had selected.

"The man who leased my boat this winter wants to buy it."

I raised a brow. "Buy it? Are you considering it?"

Danny took a sip of his beer before he answered. "He caught me off guard. Selling the boat had never entered my mind, but it's true the ol' girl needs a lot of repair and I'm getting tired of living on her. The idea of selling it and maybe getting a less seasonal job has a certain appeal, but I have no idea what I'd do to make a living. I'm not looking to leave the island, and there aren't a lot of jobs for individuals with my skill set. And if I sold the boat I'd need to find a place to live. I can't crash with Maggie full time."

Danny had owned his whale watch boat since before I graduated high school. It would seem odd for him not to have it, but I could understand why he might want a steadier revenue source.

"Is it a good offer?" Siobhan asked.

Danny nodded. "It is, actually; a very good offer. In fact, he offered me more than I would have asked for it if I'd intended to sell. And I have some money put aside for this season's startup and the repairs I planned to make once the boat came back to me. If I combined my savings with the money from the sale and found a superinexpensive place to live, I would have enough to maybe buy or even start a small business."

"You can stay with me at Mr. Parsons if Maggie kicks you out," Cody offered. "At least until you get settled."

"Thanks, man. I appreciate that."

Cody shrugged. "That's what brothers are for."

A warmth filled my heart when I realized Finn, Danny, Aiden, and Cody would all be brothers of a sort once Cody and I married. Of course, Cody and Danny had been best friends since they were young boys, so they'd probably thought of each other as brothers long before Cody and I got together.

"Okay," Siobhan said, setting down her slice on her plate and assuming the reasonable big sister role. "Say you can find a place to crash and you even manage to scrape together enough money to buy or start a business, other than whale watching or fishing, what are you qualified to do?"

"Not a lot," Danny admitted. "I can outdrink most of the guys at the bar. Do you think there's a need for something like that?" He chuckled.

Tara spoke up suddenly. "I think Danny has a lot of talents He's bright and funny and he knows how to talk to and get along with all kinds of people. He's easygoing and a hard worker who isn't afraid of long hours. He's strong and usually reliable. I think if he takes some time to look around he'll find something perfect for him."

Danny looked somewhat shocked by Tara's statement. I guess in a way I was too. They'd had a rocky romantic relationship over the years, but the friendship between them had somehow survived the starts and stops.

"I know you were kidding about being able to drink most people under the table, but what about a bar?" Finn said.

"You think Danny should open a bar?" Siobhan asked.

"I was thinking more along the lines of buying a bar. I found out today that O'Malley's is up for sale. Danny already knows all the regulars, and there's a small apartment over the bar where he could live for the time being."

A serious expression crossed Danny's face. "O'Malley's is for sale?"

"Seems to be. I went over today to talk to the bartender about a lead I was following up on and he said O'Malley had decided to sell the place and move to Boston, where his wife's family lives. O'Malley offered him the option to buy the place, but he felt like it was time for him to move on as well. I don't know how much O'Malley wants, but the bartender did say he wanted to sell to a local and was willing to make a very good deal to the right person."

Danny stood up. "I'm sorry to bail, but I really want to check this out before someone else has a chance to work out a deal with O'Malley."

"Go ahead," I said. "You can stop back when you finish if you want and it isn't too late."

"Thanks, guys. I think this might be just what I'm looking for."

With Danny gone, the conversation shifted to the weather and the spring events the island held each year. Siobhan had been working on having her job covered while she was on maternity leave and still wasn't sure what she'd do about childcare once the baby was born. While she was superexcited to be a mother and wanted to spend time with her baby, she was mayor of Madrona Island. It wasn't like she could be away from the office indefinitely. I guess I'd never stopped to consider what life would be like for Finn and Siobhan when they were parents.

It seemed the Hart family was going through a lot of transition. Cassie was graduating high school, Finn and Siobhan were having a baby, Cody and I were getting married, Danny could be changing careers, Maggie and Michael were on the way to getting married, and I had the feeling Mom and Gabe were as well. That left Aiden as the only Hart on the island not undergoing a huge change of some sort, although I wouldn't be a bit surprised if that wasn't in the future as well. Aiden was a fisherman by trade, but fishing in the area had become a lot more regulated in recent years, and he now spent most of his time in Alaska. He'd commented on more than one occasion that it might be time to rethink his life and maybe even settle down to raise a family.

After sunset we headed inside to discuss the case, or cases as they may be. We had Thea's murder to try to figure out, the tainted water in the hollow that seemed to be driving the cats away and making Tansy sick, the missing grad student, and a possible plot to orchestrate favorable conditions for the logging company on the north shore.

I looked at the whiteboard, which had taken on the look of an octopus, with lines connecting one thing to another in every which way. I supposed everything could be related, but it was equally likely they weren't.

"How did your interview with the logging operation go?" Finn asked Cody.

He twisted his lips with a look of indecision before he spoke. "I'm not sure what I took away from the meeting. Peter Billings and Sam Smart seem to be professionals. They've logged similar environments in other states and even other countries, and they seem to have a handle on what they're doing. They provided me with some pretty convincing statistics that seem to support the idea that the lack of logging on the island in recent decades has created a fire hazard. I understand the reason behind the ban on logging. The forest on the north shore was overlogged decades ago, which created a culture in which those in power were inclined to protect the trees. Additionally, the presence of the cats in the hollow was another factor to consider. I know logging in the hollow has come up in the past, and I support and understand the concept of protecting the wildlife living there."

"I sense a *but*," I said.

"But," Cody cleared this throat, "I was under the impression after speaking to them, that while they had a good business plan and had run all the numbers, they didn't have a firm grasp on what a hot-button issue logging in the hollow was bound to be. In their mind, they're doing Madrona Island a favor. They have a plan to thin the forest, greatly reducing the probability of a devastating fire at absolutely no cost to the island or its citizens. In fact, the owners of the land that will be logged are being cut in for a percentage of the profit."

"I get it," I said. "We all know there's more at stake than a fire hazard."

"Yes," Cody replied. "As I said, the data they've compiled is pretty impressive. I think once they have an opportunity to meet with the island council they're going to gain support."

"I agree," Siobhan said. "In fact, the subject of thinning the forest never died after the last time it was brought up. If a fire in an isolated location like the hollow should occur, we wouldn't have the resources to fight it. Any attempt would have to come from the air, and as you know, we don't have the helicopters needed for such an effort. The reality is, if a fire were to start in the hollow, it would probably wipe out the entire thing before it burned itself out and there wouldn't be anything anyone could do about it."

I felt a wave of nausea. In the event of a fire, where would the cats go? They'd be trapped.

"Would the outcome be the same if logging was allowed?" I asked.

"Not necessarily," Siobhan replied. "For one thing, if you reduced the amount of fuel there you'd reduce the rate at which the fire would spread. Additionally, the proposal calls for an access road into and out of the hollow. A road would make battling a smaller fire possible from the ground." Siobhan looked at me. "I know there are no easy answers, but I have to agree with Cody that sending these guys packing may not be as easy as you'd like."

Okay, this discussion had become seriously depressing. I couldn't imagine the hollow with a road through the middle of it and I certainly couldn't imagine the removal of a good percentage of the Madrona trees that gave our island its personality. On the other hand, it would be irresponsible not to consider the situation. The idea of a fire that local firefighters couldn't even begin to battle was heavy indeed.

"Okay," I said. "I can see that this is a complex subject, so let's leave solving it for another night. The real question is, do you think, after speaking to the men, that they're responsible for tainting the water in the hollow to drive the cats away?" I asked Cody.

"No. I don't. They have no reason to take such a drastic step at this point. They have a very viable plan they haven't even had the opportunity to present to the island council yet. Doing something as desperate as tainting the water supply would be extremely premature. The men I spoke to seemed to be the patient sort with a plan they'd stick to."

I rotated my shoulders to try to relieve the tension. "Assuming the logging company isn't involved, what's going on? Thea is dead, the water in the hollow has been tainted, and the grad student is missing and most likely dead. Who or what is behind this?"

No one responded, I imagined because they didn't have a clue.

"I think we need to look at each incident in isolation at least one more time before we automatically connect them," Cody said.

Finn nodded. "We've talked about Thea quite a bit, so let's switch gears and look at Travis Long. After his assistant came to the island looking for him I did some digging. Travis should have graduated from the University of Washington last year. He'd spent three years working on a project that ended up with inconclusive results. The doctoral committee couldn't accept his dissertation as presented and he was allowed another year to come up with additional information to support it. This isn't the first time he's been on the island. I found lodging records that indicate he spent time here for short periods over the past two years. This stay, which was bordering on three months, was by far the longest. He seemed to have been focusing all his energy on our water quality; he hasn't traveled to any other location since his dissertation was rejected last July."

"If his dissertation was rejected in July, what was he doing between then and three months ago, when he arrived here?" Siobhan asked.

"He made several short trips to the island between August and November and arrived in mid-December to begin his current stay. I'd imagine long-term lodging at a reasonable price could have been a problem prior to that."

"Okay, so Long has been on the island for an extended stay. I'm assuming his presence is related to whatever's going on in the hollow," Siobhan said. "It sounds like he has a lot at stake. He must have felt like he hit the lottery when he happened across the tainted water."

"Unless he's the one who tainted it," I said. "Think about it. The guy was desperate. He couldn't find in nature what he needed, so maybe he created an environment to support his hypothesis."

"Do we know what he's trying to do?" Siobhan asked.

"Beth said he's working on some sort of a water purification system that can be used in natural settings such as a lake or pond and doesn't require chemicals. I didn't really understand it, but I think it involves a filtration system."

"So he'd need a tainted water source to provide a subject for his experiment," Siobhan summed up.

"Exactly. The water in the hollow has definitely been tainted. It not only smelled bad, it appeared cloudy. Beth said the smell could be due to sulfide gas in groundwater, which could be caused by rainwater being filtered by decayed vegetation, and we've discussed the vegetation in the area being dense. The thing is, natural tainting of the water would take time, and the water was fine when I visited the hollow last summer. The only conclusion I can come to is that something's been added to the water recently, intentionally or unintentionally."

"And you're suggesting Travis tainted the water to accommodate his experiment," Siobhan said.

I shrugged. "It's possible."

"What about the wallet and the blood in his room?" Tara asked. "Both suggest he's the victim here."

"What if he wasn't assaulted? What if everything was planted?"

"Why would he want to make it appear he'd been hurt or abducted?" Tara asked.

I frowned. "I don't know why he'd fake his own abduction. It really doesn't make sense. But I think someone intentionally tainted the water; if not Travis or the men behind the logging operation, who?"

"This is giving me a headache," Siobhan said.

"Let's take a short break and then start fresh," Cody suggested.

I decided to take Max out for a quick run as long as we were taking a break. The air temperature had cooled quite a bit since the sun had set, so I put on a jacket. As soon as I opened the door Max ran out, and Apollo, who I hadn't intended to take along, ran out after him. I figured it wouldn't hurt to let the cat walk along with us, so I followed them down the beach. It was a beautiful evening, the sky clear and the air still. Unlike the huge waves we'd seen during the storm, tonight the waves rolled gently onto the sand.

One of Max's favorite things in all the world was chasing after sticks, so I picked one up and threw it down the beach. Apollo seemed content to walk by my side, and I found the tranquility of the moment did a lot to still the busyness of my mind. Life can be complicated and confusing at times, and it's nice to know I always have the calming effect of the sea to keep me from stressing out completely. I was lucky to live on the water and couldn't imagine being anywhere else. I guess I understood why Cassie wasn't more excited about going off to college. I'd felt the same way when it had come time for me to select a path for my future. I'd had a hard time getting things started, but now I had Cody and the bookstore, and life was just about perfect.

When we approached the edge of Mr. Parsons's property, where the beach turned away from the peninsula to hug the island's south shore, I paused and prepared to turn around. I called to Max, who ran back to me, but when I started walking back to the cabin Apollo didn't follow.

"Come on, kitty. It's time to get back. The others will be waiting for us."

"Meow," Apollo said before continuing in the direction in which we had originally been heading.

I sighed and took out my phone to call Cody. "I'm trying to come back, but Apollo seems to have other plans. I'd better follow him."

"Okay, but stay on the line."

"Okay. Hopefully, whatever it is he wants to show me isn't too far away."

I only needed to follow Apollo for about ten minutes before he stopped near an old pier that had rotted with age and mostly decayed. The pillars still stood and near the one farthest out in the water I noticed a dark object. I shone the flashlight from my phone toward it and then put the phone to my ear. "You'd better get Finn. I think Apollo just found Travis Long."

I sat down on the sand as a hollowness gripped my heart. I was really, really tired of all the death that seemed to find its way into my life. I knew it was somehow my calling and therefore my duty to act as a human catalyst for the cats, but there were times I was overcome with the emotions involved in such a task.

By the time Finn and Cody arrived I had shed all the tears I needed to and was ready to do whatever the situation required of me.

"He's pretty far out," Finn said.

"Mr. Parsons has a rubber raft he used to use for fishing and I use for diving," Cody offered. "I'll run there and get it. That way you can retrieve the body without getting too wet."

I stood up and walked over to where Finn was standing at water's edge.

"It's too dark to make out any details. Why did you assume the body is Travis Long?" Finn asked.

"For one thing, Apollo led me to him. For another, he's missing, so it made sense the body in the water would belong to the missing person. And I just sensed we'd found him."

Cody returned with the raft and Finn rowed out to the end of the pier. He used a rope to attach the body to the raft and then rowed back to the beach. Once the body was ashore, Finn called the main sheriff's office and reported the body. They would send someone to retrieve what was left of it.

"I pulled his photo when he was reported missing," Finn said. "I'd say based on an initial observation, this is the man from the missing persons report."

"It looks like he's been in the water for a while. Several days at least," I said.

"The medical examiner will have a better idea of time of death, but I think you're right," Finn said. "Why don't you go back and let Siobhan and Tara know what's going on?" he suggested. "I'll need to wait here until someone gets back to me about transporting the body. This most likely isn't the actual crime scene, so the sheriff might just want me to bring the remains in rather than sending someone over from San Juan Island."

"I'll go get the truck and bring it here," Cody offered.

"Thanks, I'd appreciate that."

Cody, the animals, and I set off back down the beach while Finn waited for his instructions. Life on the island was different from life in other places. More often than not, calling for backup meant waiting for reinforcements from one of the other islands. If the resident deputy could handle a situation on his own, usually he did.

"Are you sure the body you found belongs to Travis Long?" Tara asked as Cody headed off with his truck and Max, Apollo, and I went inside.

"Finn said he thought it was from a photograph he has, and I thought it was right away."

"What do you think this means?" Tara asked. "Where does it leave us? If he's another victim does that mean he wasn't the one to taint the water?"

I took a deep breath and let it out slowly. "I wish I knew. At this point all I have are questions. It feels like everything is connected, but operating under that assumption to the exclusion of all others would hinder the investigation. For now, we need to focus on answers to specific questions: Who killed Thea Blane? Who killed Travis Long, assuming he was murdered and didn't simply drown? Who's tainting the water in the hollow?"

"It's getting late," Siobhan said. "I think we should call it a night."

"I do need to get home," Tara seconded. "Should we plan to regroup tomorrow evening?"

"Sounds good to me. In the meantime, I think we should all spend some time with the three questions and jot down anything that comes to mind. Sometimes our subconscious has already figured out what our mind insists on muddying up."

Chapter 11

Friday, March 16

Who killed Thea Blane? Who killed Travis Long, assuming he was killed and didn't simply drown? Who was tainting the water in the hollow? I spent half the night pacing the cabin trying to answer those questions. Cody had helped Finn transport the body and then gone to spend the night at Mr. Parsons's house; he'd been away so much lately, he'd wanted to spend some time with him. When Siobhan and Tara left, it was only me alone with the muddy waters of my very confused brain.

I tried to get some sleep, but all I managed were a few catnaps between all the pacing. Finally, I gave up, took a shower, and got ready to face the day. The problem was, when I went to make my morning pot of coffee I realized I was completely out. The only solution was to head over to the main house to see if Finn and Siobhan were up and had made coffee. I found Siobhan sitting at the dining table in her bathrobe talking to Cassie, who was dressed for school. Happily, there was a pot of coffee on the heating tray, so I helped myself and joined them.

"You're here early," I said to Cassie. "Is everything okay?"

"Everything is fine. I just had a hard time sleeping last night, going over all the college options in my head, so I thought I'd talk to the one Hart who'd been to college to find out what she thought."

"That was a good idea." I looked at Siobhan who was sipping a glass of orange juice. "What do you think about Cassie's dilemma?"

"Personally," Siobhan said, "I couldn't wait to go to college. Mom and I were fighting, Finn was getting too serious too fast, which was making me feel trapped, and I wanted to get away from everything that was suffocating me. For me, college was my get-out-of-jail-free card. I left the island as soon after high school as I could, arguing that I needed to get set up before classes began, I met a couple of girls I had a lot in common with, joined a sorority, and the next four years were some of the best of my life. But Cassie isn't me. She loves her life here. I left to escape, but for her, leaving represents giving something up."

I turned my attention to Cassie. "Are you any closer to a decision?"

"No. I feel as confused as ever. Even if I do decide to go to college, which one, and what should I major in? The whole thing feels overwhelming."

"You don't have to choose a major right away," Siobhan said. "The first year can be about taking general education classes and finding your passion."

"I guess it would be fun to join a sorority. And I'm starting to like school. I just wish there was a college on the island, so I could go there and be home with my family and friends at the same time."

"So go to school in Seattle," Siobhan suggested. "It's close enough to come home every weekend if you want to, although once you make friends and get into the social aspect of college, I doubt you'll want to."

"And if I hate it?"

"If you try it and hate it you can quit. If you don't try it you'll always wonder."

Cassie smiled. She leaned over and hugged Siobhan. "Thanks. That helps a lot. I'm going to take another look at the University of Washington." She stood up. "I need to get to school." Cassie looked at me. "I told Tara I'd come in to help out at the bookstore after classes, so I'll see you then."

After Cassie left I poured myself a second cup of coffee. "It seems like you really helped her."

Siobhan shrugged. "I just answered the questions she asked. I think Cassie knows what she wants deep down inside, but fear of the unknown is keeping her from making a decision. She'll feel better and will probably even be excited about what the future holds once she commits."

"I could have used a big sister to talk to when I graduated high school."

Siobhan put her hand over mine. "I know. I'm sorry I wasn't here for you."

I shrugged. "It's okay. You had your own life to live and everything worked out okay." I sat back in the chair. "I noticed Finn's car is still here."

"He's upstairs on the phone. He has to run over to San Juan Island this morning. He was scheduled to testify in a deposition next week, but it got moved to today."

"The timing could be better with two murders to deal with. At least I'm assuming Travis was murdered. Did Finn say when he got home?"

"It appears Travis died from blunt force trauma to the front of the head. It's possible he was on a boat and fell, hitting his head, which made him disoriented, which caused him to fall into the water and drown, but for now he's going with murder. He should have a preliminary report from the ME later today."

I was about to respond when Finn walked into the room. "Anything new?" I asked.

"I'm having Travis Long's banking and phone records sent to me, as well as his student file from the University of Washington. I wish I didn't have to go to this deposition. I'd like to hit the ground running with this investigation."

"I have a baby doctor appointment this morning. I was planning to take the day off. If you want I can go over to your office and look through the files when they show up."

"That might be helpful," Finn said as he pulled on his jacket. "You should be able to access them off the server. You know the password. If you find anything interesting text me. I'm not sure how long the deposition will take; sometimes these things drag on and on."

"I'll call Willow to see if she can help out at the bookstore. If she can and Tara doesn't need me today I'll help with the research," I offered my sister.

"That would be great," Siobhan answered. "I'm going to run upstairs to get showered and dressed for my appointment. If you can help me just meet me at Finn's office. I should be there by ten-thirty."

I returned to my cabin and called Willow, who was fine with helping out for a few hours. I planned to take in the cats and help Tara open; Cassie would come in when she got off school at two-thirty, so Willow just needed to be there from ten-thirty to two-thirty. If it got really busy for some reason I'd just be down the street; Tara could text me and I'd come running.

I made my arrangements, took Max out for a quick run, and saw to the cats in the sanctuary. Tending the cats was a big commitment when Maggie was away; they needed to be fed and played with twice a day, and there was all the cleanup to see to as well. Cody helped when he was around, but he had a lot on his plate as well, so I hated to ask. Perhaps I should talk to Danny about helping. He wasn't really a cat person, but he wasn't working at the moment, and he was living in Maggie's house for free. He had the time and I didn't suppose it was an absolute requirement that you love cats to feed them and clean a few cat boxes.

After everyone had been fed and played with I started loading the cats I planned to take to the cat lounge today. I had a black feral who had been grumpy when he first arrived, but I had been spending extra time with him and felt he might be ready for a forever home if I could find the right person. On a whim, I decided to take him with me today and was loading him into the car when Danny pulled into the drive behind me.

"Where did you come from?" I asked. "I didn't even know you were gone. I just assumed you were still asleep."

"No time for sleep," Danny said with a huge grin on his face.

"I take it your meeting with O'Malley went well last night."

"He had one other person interested in the bar, but I think we came to a very workable solution."

I slid the crate I was holding into the backseat. "Oh, and what solution is that?"

"The other guy and I are going to be partners. We're each going to put up half the money and provide half the oversight. He already has an apartment, so he was fine with letting me have the space over the bar."

I frowned. "Are you sure about this? Business partnerships can be tricky. Tara and I are best friends and we still had some issues to work out when we first started working together."

"I'm sure. I've known this guy my whole life. I think I know what to expect from him."

I raised a brow. "Who is it?"

"Aiden."

"Our brother Aiden?"

"One and the same." Danny's grin grew even larger. "Isn't it great?"

I wasn't sure. I loved both Danny and Aiden. They were fantastic people and wonderful brothers, but they tended to fight over pretty much everything the entire time we were growing up. Of course, Aiden and Siobhan fought all the time too, so I guessed it was a sibling thing, and it had gotten better once they were older and no longer living together. Still, they were so different. I wasn't sure how this would work out.

Aiden was the oldest, and as the oldest, he assumed he was the boss and his opinion was the only one that mattered. Danny was a pretty easygoing guy who usually let Aiden have his way rather than argue with him. But with his money and livelihood on the line, I wasn't sure that was going to be the case in the future. And even more important, while Aiden was serious—timely, methodical, and detail oriented—Danny had a laxer approach to life. Danny lived in a world where time commitments were approximations and doing something pretty well was more than well enough.

"I don't know, Danny. I love you both and want you to be happy and successful, but you're so different."

"You're kick back and easygoing like me and Tara is focused and organized like Aiden and you make it work."

"That's true. But I can't help but wonder what will happen the first time you're supposed to open at four and don't show up until four twenty."

Danny frowned. "I know I have a relaxed approach to timeliness, but I realize I'll have to change. I'm going to be a business owner. I'll need to think and act like one."

"You've been a business owner, but you showed up to charters late all the time," I pointed out.

"Okay, I get it. Aiden isn't going to put up with me being a slacker. The obvious answer is not to be one. I really want to do this, Cait. Aiden really wants to do it. Be happy for us."

Working out Aiden and Danny's lives wasn't my job; I let out a breath and smiled. "Okay." I hugged Danny. "Congratulations. Is this a for-sure thing?"

"We still need to work out a few things, but we have a verbal commitment with O'Malley. I still need to sell my boat and Aiden needs to sell his. As long as there are no hitches, I should have the money from mine in a couple of weeks, so I'll be able to give O'Malley the deposit while Aiden sells his boat. O'Malley really does want to sell to a local who won't do anything to drive away the regulars, so he's willing to wait for us to get our finances together. He's even willing to finance part of it himself if we don't come up with enough cash."

"It sounds like you have a good plan. Just be sure to really talk to Aiden before you commit to make sure you're on the same page."

Danny kissed my cheek. "I will. I promise."

I was about to close the car door when Danny stopped me. "Is that Whiskey?"

I looked at the black cat. "You mean the cat?"

"Yeah. I know you've been calling him Midnight or something, but I like Whiskey. Are you going to adopt him out?"

"To the right person. He's not one to want to cuddle, or even to be touched much, but he no longer bites or scratches when approached, so I thought I'd test the waters."

"Can you hold him for me? If this all works out and I get my own pad an independent cat who doesn't want to cuddle will be a perfect pet for me."

"Really? Are you sure? He'll still need to be fed and cleaned up after."

"I'm sure. I've been hanging out with the cats during the day when you and Siobhan are at work. I've never been a cat person, but Whiskey and I have bonded. We roll to the same drummer."

"I think its *march* to the same drummer."

"Whatever. Will you hold him?"

I lifted the cat carrier out of the car. "Okay. I'll hold him for you. The more I think about it, the more I think you really are perfect for each other."

I dropped the other cats off in the cat lounge and caught Tara up on the latest development with Danny and Aiden. She thought it was a wonderful idea and wasn't concerned in the least about the differences between them. I pointed out that Aiden's tendency to be overly serious combined with Danny's go-with-the-flow approach to life didn't necessarily mesh, and she insisted that my brothers were intelligent men capable of making the adjustments necessary to make the enterprise a success. Go figure. I was usually the one with the don't-worry-be-happy approach, while Tara liked to plan and control everything. We seemed to have switched personalities.

Chapter 12

"I think I may have found something in Travis's student file," I said to Siobhan. We'd spent the past two hours looking through all the documents Finn had requested, but until now we'd come up empty.

Siobhan tossed the file she'd been looking through on the table. "Great. Because I haven't."

"When Travis was given an additional year to complete his research he also got a bill for an extra year's tuition and housing. I found a note from Travis to the business office letting them know his student loans had run dry and he'd need some time to get the money together. They gave him until classes started in September to make a down payment, with the next larger payment due by the end of the calendar year. According to this, Travis's tuition and housing was paid in full in December." I looked up at Siobhan. "When I looked through his banking records I noticed he seemed to be pretty broke. I certainly didn't notice a lump sum either going in or going out, so the money to pay for his schooling had to have come from somewhere other than his checking account. Even a loan would have been paid out to him and he would have written a check to the school. I thought about it and realized a parent or other relative might have helped him out and paid the school directly, so I went back and traced the payment back to its source. It came from a private party."

"Okay, who paid the tuition?"

"A man named Mark Benson."

"Why does that name sound familiar?" Siobhan asked.

"Drake Benson is one of the partners in Caldwell and Benson. Perhaps Mark Benson and Drake Benson are related."

"Let's find out," Siobhan suggested.

After twenty minutes of surfing the web we were able to confirm that Mark Benson was Drake Benson's brother. Mark had a son named Devon who also attended the University of Washington. A call to Travis's assistant, Beth, provided us with the information that Devon and Travis had been roommates. She hadn't been aware that Devon's father had paid Travis's tuition, but she did say Devon's family had money, and the two men were really close.

"What if Cody is wrong about the logging firm and they *are* the ones who tainted the water and drove the cats away? What if they spoke to their attorney about the cats and someone from Caldwell and Benson suggested they find a way to drive away the cats without making the water toxic? Maybe Drake mentioned the situation to his father, who might have met Travis on occasion, and he called Travis to work out a deal to taint the water in return for the money he needed to pay his tuition."

"Seems like a long shot and kind of convoluted."

"Maybe it didn't happen exactly that way. But the link seems to be Caldwell and Benson. Thea was fired while temping for them, we believed because she saw something she shouldn't. The logging company was working with Caldwell and Benson on their project. Driving the cats away would remove a roadblock, and the water just happened to turn up tainted. Travis knows all about water and pollutants and desperately needs money. He just happened to be roommates with Drake Benson's nephew. It's a sloppy theory, but the dots do connect."

"So how do we prove it?"

I drummed my fingers on the table. "I don't know. Maybe Finn can obtain information we don't have access to. Or maybe he can get the logging guys to 'fess up and admit what they did."

Siobhan looked doubtful. "Say this theory is right. Why kill Travis?"

I leaned back in the chair and crossed my arms over my chest. "Maybe he grew a conscience and threatened to tell?"

"I suppose it could have gone down that way."

Siobhan texted Finn with an abbreviated version of my theory. He texted back to say he was almost done on San Juan Island and would stop off to have a chat with Peter Billings and Sam Stuart from the logging operation on his way back. He suggested someone should have a conversation with Devon Benson. He'd call to have Seattle PD handle the interview.

"What do you think?" I asked Siobhan. "Is there more to find with the information we have?"

"Probably not. Let's grab some lunch. I'm starving."

"By the way, how did your doctor appointment go?" I asked as we neatly stacked the files we had copied on Finn's desk.

"It went well. I hope the baby comes early. I'm excited to be a mother, but I'm done with this whole pregnancy thing. As far as I'm concerned, Connor can't get here soon enough."

"They say the last trimester is the hardest, but it should go fast."

Siobhan put her hand on her belly. "I hope so. Right now, three months seems like a lifetime. Of course, I'd hoped we'd be settled in our own home before he came so I could have the nursery all set up."

"Still haven't found what you want?"

Siobhan shook her head. "Finn wants four or more bedrooms and I want to be close to our jobs and the water. We both don't want to overspend, but the houses that meet our requirements are way over our budget. Staying with Maggie has been fine. She hasn't been home a lot and her house is close to both town and the water. At some point we're going to have to find our own place."

I put my arm around Siobhan's shoulders. "Don't worry. The perfect house is out there just waiting for you. In the meantime, I've enjoyed having you close. It's been so nice that you and Finn are just across the lawn."

"It has been fun," Siobhan agreed. "Of course, eventually you'll be moving out to live with Cody.

Too bad the cabin isn't bigger; it would be perfect for us in terms of location."

"Hey, keep your nesting instinct away from my cabin. I'm not ready to move out yet."

Siobhan turned and looked at me. "You aren't having doubts, are you?"

"What? Of course not. Why would you even ask that?"

"You've been engaged for five months and you haven't set a date or made a single decision regarding the wedding."

"Five months isn't all that long. And we've had a lot of things to deal with. We're both committed to spending our lives together; we just aren't in a rush to dive into all the planning that's required. It isn't going to be pretty."

Siobhan frowned. "What do you mean by that?"

"Cody's mother wants us to get married in Florida. In fact, she's been quite insistent on it. She wanted us to get married this winter, but Cody managed to put the brakes on that idea, though she isn't giving up on the Florida idea."

"But your entire family is here."

"And his entire family is there. There are a couple of elderly relatives, including Cody's grandfather, who aren't in good enough health to make the trip here. I understand her concern, but every time I even begin to think about trying to find a solution I start to hyperventilate. I just can't deal with it right now. Maybe we'll just elope."

"That might not be a bad idea given the situation, but if you do Mom will kill you. Probably literally. And I'm pregnant, so I don't know that I can protect you the way I did when we were kids and she came after you with that wooden spanking spoon she kept in her purse."

I smiled at Siobhan's attempt at humor even though her warning wasn't all that far off. My mom might not do me physical harm, but she wouldn't be happy. "Let's talk about happier things and leave wedding planning to another time. I know you want to wait to buy furniture for the nursery until you have a place of your own, but you know you're having a boy, so how about if we head over to the baby store after lunch and buy Connor a couple of outfits?"

Siobhan smiled. "I'd love that. I've been envisioning a sailor suit with a white sailor hat ever since I found out we were having a boy."

"Like the photo of Dad that Mom has. He sure was a cute kid. I bet Connor will inherit something from him. Maybe his eyes."

"I'd love for Connor to have Dad's eyes as long as he has Finn's smile."

"And your hair," I added. It was kind of fun to play build a baby.

******

I was at the bookstore helping Tara restock when my cell rang. "Hey, Finn, what's up?"

"I spoke to Peter Billings and Sam Stuart. They claim to know nothing about the tainted water in the hollow, and I believe them. Cody was right when he said they'd done their homework and had a solid proposal to present to the island council. They did say they weren't aware of the problem with the cats. They hired Caldwell and Benson to help them with the permit process and to anticipate any push back from the local population, and according to both of them, the only problem the law firm presented to them had to do with the intrinsic value a lot of the local population places on the Madrona trees for which the island is named."

"Okay, so if they didn't hire Travis to taint the water why did Mark Benson pay Travis's tuition?"

"I'm not sure yet. According to the officer who interviewed Devon, he wasn't aware that his father had paid Travis's tuition, though he admitted Travis had been to his home many times and he and his father had a good relationship. Devon suspects Travis may have spoken to his father about his financial issues. I have a call in to Mark Benson. I guess I should have just spoken to him directly in the first place."

"If the guys from the logging firm didn't taint the water who did? And more importantly, who killed Travis?"

Finn sighed. "I don't know. I do have some good news. I spoke to Travis's adviser about the problem he was having with his project. I hoped having a better understanding of the issues would help me understand why Travis might be involved in the tainting of the water in the hollow. I explained about the rotten-egg smell you noticed and the adviser said the smell does come from sulfide gas. He said adding sulfur to the water in the hollow wouldn't help Travis all that much because sulfur in groundwater is a common and easily remedied problem. I asked about a remedy and he said if the water was chemically altered, as we suspect, he had a filtration system that would counteract the chemicals that may have been added. He would need to test the water to see exactly what was going on, but he felt our water problem would provide a teaching opportunity, so he offered to bring some students to the island tomorrow to test, filter, and clean up the contaminated water."

"That *is* good news. Maybe once the water is clear the cats will come back."

"I'm on my way back to the island. Maybe we should meet again this evening."

"I think everyone is coming to the cabin. I'll pick up some meat to barbecue."

After I hung up I called Tansy to give her the good news about the water. She was happy the problem would be dealt with, but like the rest of us, she was concerned about the fact that we didn't seem to be making progress with Thea's murder, and the second one she'd just heard about. She asked if I was providing Apollo with adequate opportunity to show me what I needed to find, and I admitted I'd been busy and hadn't spent as much time with him as I probably should have. I promised to make a point of working with him that evening.

"Did Finn have news?" Tara asked.

I filled her in on what he'd shared with me.

"So if Travis didn't taint the water who did?" Tara asked.

I paused to consider that question. Finn had said Travis's adviser didn't think sulfur in the water or the presence of sulfide gas would help Travis with his project. I supposed that eliminated the project as a motive for Travis to have tainted the water, but despite what Devon had told the officer he spoke to, it still seemed like money for tuition was as good a motive as any. And if the motive was to drive the cats away but not to kill them, as seemed to be the case, whoever was behind the whole thing would need someone who understood the cause and effect of chemical additives to the water system.

"I'm still liking Travis for the one to taint the water. Cody and Finn both feel the logging operators weren't involved in the water issue, and they both have good instincts. If not the loggers, we need to ask ourselves who else would benefit from the cats leaving."

"The property owners," Tara said. "Cody said the loggers planned to compensate the landowners for the trees that were taken from their land by giving them a percentage of the profits. If the cats become an issue, as we both know they will, the logging company will move onto another area and the landowners will lose the potential for what I assume would be a pretty significant payday."

"Nora Bradley owns the land in the hollow. I know she's been struggling since Mayor Bradley was killed, and I imagine income from the logging operation would be welcome. I could even see her being behind the removal of the cats from the hollow via nonlethal means. But even if she was the one to hire Travis, I don't see her being the one to kill him."

"Yeah, that part doesn't fit," Tara admitted. "Do we know who owns the land on the north end of the island that was to be logged as well?"

I shook my head. "I don't know, but I can find out." I called Cody and asked him if he could get the information. He said he could and would. I told him about my plan to barbecue that evening, which he thought was great. The warm weather had held, and I imagined he would welcome the chance to be outdoors for a bit after spending the entire day inside at the newspaper office.

I called Danny and Siobhan and told them about our plans for the evening. Cassie was still at the bookstore and I invited her to join us. With my calls finished, I spoke to her about bringing the cats back to the sanctuary after the store closed, then said my good-byes and headed out. I mulled over the mysteries the group had been grappling with while I picked out thick steaks, fresh asparagus, and ingredients for salad. By the time I got home I'd come to the conclusion that the missing piece in our investigation was Travis's girlfriend. When I had taken Travis's wallet to Finn he'd mentioned she was the one who had reported him missing, though Beth had seemed positive Travis didn't have a girlfriend. Maybe this mystery girlfriend knew why Travis had been spending so much time on the island if the water in the hollow really wouldn't work for the project he ought to have been spending all his time on.

Chapter 13

Cody had the steaks on the grill by the time everyone arrived. It was another beautiful evening, so we enjoyed the food and the weather before we jumped into murder talk. It was nice to spend time with my family and friends, and while I really did hope Finn and Siobhan found their dream house, I was loving the additional time their closeness provided.

"Anything new with the purchase of the bar?" I asked Danny after we'd all served ourselves and gathered around the picnic table.

"I called the man who's renting my boat to say I'm interested in selling and he's getting a sales contract together. He has cash on hand; once the details are worked out and the contract is signed he can pay me right away. O'Malley's good with the money I'll get from the sale as a down payment, so we're moving forward with a sales agreement between him and Aiden and me. Aiden still needs to sell his boat, but this is a good time of year for that, so hopefully things will move along quickly."

"Does Mom know about this?" Cassie asked.

"No, and I prefer you not mention it until Aiden and I have a chance to sit her down to explain things. She'll probably feel nostalgic that Aiden is selling the boat he inherited from Dad, but I think she'll be happy to have him here on Madrona for the whole year instead of just part of it."

"She'll be thrilled," Cassie agreed. "She's been wanting Aiden to settle down and have a family. Now maybe he will."

"He's not even dating anyone," I said.

"I wouldn't be so sure about that," Cassie said with a tone in her voice that indicated she knew something I didn't.

"Okay, spill. What do you know?" I asked my younger sister.

"Let's just say I've seen Aiden twice in as many months dining at Antonio's with a certain redheaded Irish girl Mom already loves like one of her own daughters."

"Aiden is dating Alanna?" Alanna Quinn was the daughter of one of our mother's best friends, Julianna Quinn. If Aiden and Alanna did hook up both Mom and Julianna would be over-the-moon happy.

"Based on the fact that they were looking so intently at each other that they didn't even notice my friends and me sitting across the restaurant, I'd say their relationship has taken on an intimate aspect."

I looked at Danny. "Did you know about this?"

Danny shrugged. "Aiden might have mentioned something, but it seems obvious he isn't ready to bring the family into his relationship, so I suggest you girls keep this to yourselves until he is."

"What do you mean, us girls?" Siobhan complained. "Aren't you worried Finn and Cody will blab?"

"Not even a tiny bit. Now, can we get back to the bar?"

"I bet Alanna is the reason Aiden was interested in the bar in the first place," I said with a grin. "I've had a feeling for quite a while now that there might be something going on between those two other than friendship."

"I wonder how long it's been going on," Siobhan mused. "Aiden and Alanna have been friends since they were toddlers. If they're having a romance, it must seem so weird."

"So back to the bar…" Danny suggested for the second time.

"Are you thinking of changing anything?" Cody asked.

"We are thinking of making some small changes," Danny answered. "Nothing major that will scare off the regulars, but Aiden and I both agree the bar needs to have a larger beer selection, with a focus on regional microbrews. We want to add a larger selection of whiskey as well."

"Do you think the employees will make the transition to sign on with you?" Finn asked.

"I don't see why not," Danny said. "Aiden and I both spend a lot of time at O'Malley's during the winter. We know all the employees and we get along with everyone. I'm hoping for a totally seamless transition."

I hoped so as well, though I'd learned that few things in life were as problem free as we hoped they'd be.

After we'd eaten, Cody and Cassie tackled the dishes while Finn returned some calls, Tara and Siobhan chatted about baby clothes, and Danny and I headed to the cat sanctuary. I hadn't been sure if Aiden and Danny going into business was a good idea when I'd first heard, but now that I had a larger picture of what was going on in both men's lives, I could see buying the bar together might be a good move for both my brothers.

"If you want to feed everyone I'll start on the cat boxes," I said as Danny and I entered the sanctuary.

"I need to say hi to Whiskey first."

I watched in stunned silence as Danny entered the main cat room. Midnight, or Whiskey, as Danny was calling him, trotted right over and sat in front of him. He said something to the cat before lowering his hand. The cat responded by placing his paw on Danny's hand and then quickly removing it.

"You taught him to high five?" I asked.

Danny reached into his pocket and took out a salmon treat. He gave it to the cat, who took it and ran off to eat it. "Technically, it was a low five, but yeah. It's the way Whiskey and I show our affection without all the hugging and baby talk."

Suddenly I felt like I'd been transported to another dimension, where everything was upside down and inside out. If Danny and Cassie were correct, it looked like Aiden might be dating his childhood buddy, who we called Alanna but he called Al, and Danny, who had never been one to commit to anything or anyone, was talking about getting a pet.

When the cats were taken care of we washed up and returned to the cabin, where Siobhan had set up the whiteboard. Cody and Cassie were finishing up the dishes and Finn was walking back toward the cabin from the main house, where he'd gone to make his calls. As soon as we'd all gathered, Finn jumped right in.

"I just spoke to Mark Benson, who informed me that the reason he paid Travis's tuition was because of a deal he made with his son."

"A deal?" I asked.

"It seems Mr. Benson has been trying to get his son to agree to work in the family business for a year before going off on his own, but up to that point Devon had refused. Mr. Benson said Devon came to him last fall with a proposal. He'd work for his dad for a year when he graduated before doing anything on his own if he'd pay his roommate's tuition. Mr. Benson said he'd met Travis in the past and he seemed like a good kid, so he didn't mind helping him out. He accepted his son's proposal."

"So Devon lied?" I asked.

"It sounds like it," Finn agreed. "He did tell the officer who interviewed him that he had no idea his dad had paid his roommate's tuition, and it appears it was his idea all along."

"What about the girlfriend?" I asked. "Did you track her down?"

"The person who reported Travis missing is a local girl named Marie Trainor. I spoke to her this afternoon and she said she met Travis shortly before Christmas. Apparently, she and Travis had been dating ever since. He was supposed to take her out this past weekend, but he never showed. When she didn't hear from him by Monday she called in the missing persons report."

"Marie Trainor owns the land on the north end of the island that the logging company is interested in," Cody said. "She inherited it from her grandfather two years ago. It seems not only is the logging company interested in her trees but there's a home developer who might be interested in buying the land once the trees are cleared out."

"Sounds like Marie had a motive to want the cats gone and a boyfriend with the know-how to make it so," I said.

Finn stood up. "It seems Ms. Trainor and I need to have another conversation."

After Finn left we all sat around not talking about much of anything. It felt like we'd figured out who tainted the water and why. But who killed Travis? Marie? Had he perhaps had second thoughts and she decided to eliminate the possibility that he would tell what he knew? Or had someone else killed Travis for an entirely different reason altogether?

"What now?" Siobhan eventually asked. "Do we keep working on this or wait to see what Finn finds out?"

"Let's assume Travis did taint the water in the hollow to help Marie. Let's even assume Marie knew about what he was doing. We still don't know who killed him, and let's not forget this whole thing started with us trying to find out who killed Thea. I say we work on those questions while Finn confirms the water-tainting part of the mystery."

"If Travis decided to taint the water in the hollow to help Marie and the Bensons aren't part of it, why did Devon lie about the reason his father paid

Travis's tuition? It makes no sense to lie. He could have told the officer he asked his dad to pay Travis's tuition. And for that matter, why make the deal at all?" Tara asked. "It sounded like he had to promise his dad he'd do something he very much didn't want to do to get the money for Travis. Why would he go to that length to help him, even if they were friends?"

"Good question," I responded. "It does seem Devon went above and beyond for Travis. There must be more going on than we realize."

"So what do we do?" Danny asked. "I doubt asking the guy why he lied will get us the answers we need."

"Other than his name and the fact that he's Drake Benson's nephew, what do we know about Devon Benson?" Cody asked.

"That he was Travis's roommate. They seemed to be close. Could they have been studying similar fields?"

Cody got up from where he'd been sitting on the sofa, went over to the dining table, and booted up my laptop. After a minute he typed in some commands and we all waited. I assumed he was digging around in Devon Benson's life.

"According to an interview conducted by the campus newspaper, Devon was planning to go into environmental law," Cody informed us several minutes later. "Devon is an undergrad in the middle of his junior year, and at twenty-one, he's quite a bit younger than Travis, who was twenty-six."

"I wonder how an undergrad and a grad student ended up as roommates," Tara said.

Cody looked at me. "Do you still have Travis's student file?"

"Finn has it in the main house," Siobhan said. "It's on the desk in the guest room."

"I'll go and grab it," Danny offered. "Anything else while I'm over there?"

"The chocolate ice cream in the freezer," Siobhan responded.

I took Max out for a quick walk while there was a lull in the conversation. Apollo followed us to the door, so I let him come along. I didn't want to miss anything, so I planned for this to be a short walk, but both animals seemed to appreciate my effort.

"We don't have a lot of time, so do what you need to do," I instructed Max, who was busy running up and down the beach. He had been cooped up all day; I didn't blame him for being hyper in the evening. Unlike Max, who had a lot of pent-up energy, Apollo seemed content to walk along beside me as I strolled down the beach. I'd hoped to have some time tonight to prompt him into leading me to a clue in Thea's death, but so far, the discussion had been all about Travis and the water in the hollow. It was looking less and less like Thea's death and whatever was going on with Travis were related, but I supposed it was still a possibility we should consider. There were some connections. Thea had worked for and been fired by Caldwell and Benson; Benson's nephew had been Travis's roommate and his brother had paid Travis's tuition. There was talk that Thea might have been attempting to blackmail someone using information she found during one of her temp jobs. She'd been asking questions about legal statutes and Caldwell and Benson were attorneys. There didn't seem to be an obvious link between the two murders, but my gut told me that we should continue to dig around beneath the surface.

I looked down to inform Apollo that we'd be turning around and realized he was no longer beside me. I stopped walking and looked around. "Apollo," I called. Max had come running, but I still didn't see the cat. "Here, kitty. Where are you? It's dark and I can't see you."

"Meow," I heard from a distance.

The sound was coming from the direction in which we had just traveled, so I turned around and called to the cat once more. I still didn't see him, but Max seemed to know where to find him. I followed him to a rock grouping that was beneath the waterline during high tide but exposed during low. Low tide wouldn't be for another couple of hours, though the tide was out far enough that the rocks were accessible from the beach side.

"What'd you find?" I asked the cat.

The way the rocks were formed often trapped items from the sea; heavy items settled into the sand, while lighter objects were washed back out with the next tide. At first, I wasn't sure what Apollo was looking at; I thought it was a log but then realized it was a bat. Thea and Travis had both been hit with blunt objects. Could Apollo have just found the murder weapon used in one of the murders?

I picked up the bat and headed back to the house. Finn should be able to match the bat to the wound. He'd also be able to check for any blood residue that might have survived the ocean. If this bat was used in a murder, chances were Finn could prove it.

Chapter 14

Saturday, March 17

When Finn had returned the previous evening he'd told us that Marie had admitted Travis was the one who tainted the water in the hollow. She hadn't known what he'd done at first, but he'd confessed to her that he'd been adding chemicals that wouldn't harm the cats but would drive them away when they spoke just two days before he disappeared. She also told Finn that while she appreciated Travis's effort to help her, she didn't want to do anything illegal, so he'd promised to clean up the water before anyone found out. It was her belief that he'd gone to the hollow on the day he'd disappeared to undo what he'd done.

Finn asked Marie about Travis's relationship with Devon and the money he'd apparently helped him raise, but she said she knew very little about him before he came to Madrona Island. The only thing Travis had told her was that he'd been involved in a relationship before he'd come to the island and he felt it was time for a change.

This was the first mention of Travis having been in a serious relationship. When I'd mentioned to Beth that Travis's girlfriend had reported him missing her response was that he didn't have a girlfriend. If Travis had been in a serious relationship wouldn't his student assistant have known about it? This ex of his might be worthwhile tracking down.

While we'd waited for Finn we'd gone through Travis's student file again. It looked like he and Devon had gotten a room together Travis's third year of grad school and Devon's sophomore year as an undergrad. I guessed they must have met and become friends the previous year. When Travis was required to do another year, the pair decided to maintain their living arrangements.

I woke early the next morning and headed out to see to the cats. I hoped to finish my chores early enough to take Max for a long run before I had to go in to work. I was just finishing up in the cat sanctuary when my phone rang. I didn't recognize the number. "Hello?"

"Cait, it's Beth."

"How are you, Beth? I've thought about you often since finding out about Travis. I knew you'd take the news that Travis's body had been found as hard as anyone."

"I do miss Travis. I still can't believe he's really gone. The reason I'm calling is because I know something that probably isn't relevant to what happened to Travis, but in light of everything, I decided I should share."

"Okay. I'm listening."

"When we met last you told me that Travis's girlfriend had reported him missing. At the time I told you that he didn't have a girlfriend."

"But he did?"

"No, I didn't lie. In the six months I knew Travis he didn't have a girlfriend. But he was in a relationship. A pretty serious one."

I frowned as I tried to sort things out. "Travis had a boyfriend," I realized.

"He'd been involved in a long-term relationship with his roommate, Devon Benson. I maybe should have told you right away, but we didn't know Travis was dead and he was really private about his sexual orientation. I didn't want to betray his trust. Most people just thought they were close friends."

"Did Travis ever say anything to you about breaking things off with Devon?"

"He did. The last time we spoke on the phone I asked him how Devon felt about him being away so long. He said he'd met someone else and had decided to break things off with Devon. I don't know for sure he did it before he went missing, but I suspect he did. I ran into Devon a week ago Friday and he was in a really bad mood. He told me he needed to get away and was going home for the weekend."

Suddenly everything, or almost everything, fell into place. "Thanks, Beth. This helps a lot. I have to go now, but I'll call you back when I can talk longer."

I headed to the main house. Finn and Siobhan were sitting at the kitchen table having coffee. At least Finn was having coffee. Siobhan seemed to be drinking hot cider. "I think I know who killed Travis," I said after pouring my own cup of coffee.

"Who?" Siobhan asked before Finn had a chance to.

"Devon Benson."

"Why would Devon Benson kill Travis?" Finn asked. "They were friends."

"They were more than friends," I offered. "I just spoke to Beth and she told me that Devon and Travis had been involved in a romantic relationship. It all makes perfect sense. Devon was in love with Travis. Travis was in a tight spot financially and might get kicked out of school, so Devon sold his soul to the devil, making the ultimate sacrifice by agreeing to work for his dad for a year upon graduation in exchange for the money Travis needed. Travis then came here and met Marie. He fell in love with her and began spending more and more time on the island, the whole time telling everyone he was here doing research. Beth told me that when she spoke to Travis last week he confided in her that he had met someone and planned to break if off with Devon. She also said she ran into Devon a week ago Friday and was in a dark mood. He told her he needed a break and was going home for the weekend."

"Only he didn't go home; he came to the island and confronted Travis," Siobhan finished. "He had, after all, made the ultimate sacrifice out of love for a man who'd thrown that love back in his face."

"Exactly," I said. I looked at Finn. "I bet if you check you'll find Devon rented a boat over the weekend. And if you check his credit card records I bet you'll find transactions in the area."

Finn stood up. "I like your theory. I'll head into the office and check it out."

"What did you find out about the bat?" I asked.

"I sent it to the ME. He thinks there's a good chance we'll find a match. I'll let you know when I find out for sure."

******

"Wow I never once thought Travis's death would turn out to be the result of love gone wrong. It's a crazy world we live in," Tara said.

After I'd left Finn and Siobhan I'd taken Max for a run as planned and then cleaned up and came to the store.

"Finn called to say the Seattle PD have picked up Devon, who pretty much confessed to everything. We started off trying to solve Thea's murder, stumbled onto the situation with Travis, and got sidetracked. Now that we've figured out why the water in the hollow was tainted and who killed Travis, we should get back to Thea's murder."

"I've almost forgot where we left things," Tara admitted.

"The last I recall we'd eliminated Pam Wilkins and Victoria Grace. Danny talked to John Walkman, who said he didn't do it, but we both agreed he should stay on the list. In addition to John Walkman, another love interest of Thea's, Walter Bodine, was added to the list just before we became distracted by Travis's death. And there was reason to believe Thea may have stumbled on to sensitive information that she planned to use in a blackmail scheme, making the blackmail target as well as Caldwell and Benson suspects."

"Okay, that gets us back to where we were. We just need to eliminate each of the five until we're left with only one."

"In my opinion the subject of the blackmail scheme seems to have the most motive. Finn didn't find any evidence that Thea received any money despite mentioning to several people that she was about to come into some. I think her blackmail demand was met with violence."

Tara poured a cup of coffee for each of us. "How do we figure out who she planned to blackmail?"

"I suppose someone from Caldwell and Benson would know. She was fired for snooping, so she must have been caught in the act. Siobhan said there's a man named Bruce Wong working in the local office. It's Saturday, so I imagine they're closed, but I'm sure Finn could track him down. I'll call him."

Finn agreed speaking to Bruce might be a good idea. Danny knew John Walkman better than any of us, so I called him and suggested he buy him a drink to get more out of him than he had during their last meeting. That left Lilly Kent and Walter Bodine. I didn't know Walter, but I did know Lilly, so I was going to start there. Cassie was due to come in to the store later in the morning, so I figured Tara should be fine if I took an hour out of my day to buy Lilly a cup of coffee.

"I imagine you want to talk to me about Thea," Lilly jumped right in as soon as she arrived at Coffee Café.

"What makes you say that?"

"I've known you for what, fifteen years? And never once in those years have you asked me out for coffee. You have a reputation for helping that cute brother-in-law of yours, so let's save some time. I hated Thea Blane. As far as I was concerned, she was the one unscalable wall between me and the relationship I should have had with Steve. They'd been divorced for years, but it was obvious they still loved each other. She'd call the house two or three times a week needing help with one thing or another and Steve would go running. I knew deep down in my heart that as long as she was in the picture he would never be truly mine, but I didn't kill her."

"Do you have an alibi for last Saturday?"

"Isn't that a question Finn should be asking?"

"Yes, I guess it is," I admitted.

Lilly handed me a business card. "This is the contact information for my masseuse. I was with her from eleven until twelve-thirty on Saturday." Lilly handed me a second card. "This is the number for my hairdresser. My appointment started at one and went until about three. Then I met my friend Leia for drinks. We were together until six, at which time I met Steve for dinner. While I suppose it's possible I could have stopped by Thea's between appointments, I didn't. Now, if you'll excuse me, I need to go."

She stood up and left. I guess she'd told me, and I suppose I didn't blame her. I was about to accuse her of murder. Her comment did make me wonder why Finn hadn't interviewed her. I took out my phone and called him.

"Hey, Cait, what's up?"

"I just spoke to Lilly Kent. I don't think she killed Thea."

"I know. I cleared her days ago."

"It would have been nice if you'd mentioned it."

"I'm sorry. I guess it just slipped my mind. Her name hasn't come up since that first night. I guess we should update the suspect list now that we have Travis's murder solved."

"Okay, who do you have?" I asked.

"Just the blackmail victim, if the rumors are true and she really did try to blackmail someone."

"Did you speak to Bruce Wong?"

"I did, and he told me Thea was fired for making copies of documents from client files. When he caught her, she was making copies of a file belonging to Samantha Erwin. It seems Samantha is being sued by one of her clients over a bad haircut."

"A bad haircut? You can be sued for something like that?"

"You can be sued for anything. In this case, the client claimed the haircut was so bad it prevented her from getting a job she was qualified for and would have been hired if not for it. Samantha is claiming her customer brought in a photo and she gave her exactly what she asked for. Both women are furious, and it looks like it may go to court, but I spoke to both Samantha and the customer and neither of them seemed to know who Thea was."

"Is it possible Thea looked at other files she wasn't caught copying?"

"Very possible. Bruce didn't know off hand what she might have stumbled on to, but he said he'd review his client files to see if anything stood out. I mentioned to him that Thea was asking about local codes relating to the manipulation of the environment."

"So unless we can figure out who Thea was trying to blackmail, we probably won't be able to identify her killer."

"We don't know for certain she was killed by an intended blackmail victim, but even if she was, we have other means of uncovering clues that aren't readily apparent. Look, I gotta go. I'll talk to you later."

I didn't see what more I could do at that point, so I headed back to the bookstore. I suppose I could have tried to track down Walter Bodine, but I didn't know him, and we should all really compare notes before we did more so we didn't waste time interviewing the same people, as I had with Lilly. When I got there Tara told me that she and Cassie had things handled if I wanted to go home early, and I took her up on her offer.

I took Max and Apollo down to the beach. It was a warm, sunny day, and I felt I needed some time to process things and come up with a plan. The fact that we'd eliminated all named suspects and were left with an unnamed blackmail victim was progress, I supposed, but where did we go from there? Finn was certain Samantha Ervin hadn't killed Thea, and while I didn't know her well, I tended to agree. Not only did I not consider her to be aggressive, but the lawsuit seemed to be pretty cut and dried. I didn't see how there could be any secrets buried within the notes in that file in the law office that would be worth killing over.

Which led me to wonder why Thea was copying those notes in the first place. I supposed one could argue that Samantha might not want news of her lawsuit circulating around town. Even the suggestion that the haircut she'd given was so bad it had cost a customer a job could be damaging to her business, though I still didn't think it was so scandalous as to be blackmail-worthy. There had to be something more.

I picked up a stick and tossed it down the beach for Max. Apollo, as usual, seemed happy to trot along next to me. "You know," I said to him, "I just realized the key word here is *copy*. Thea was caught copying files. Sure, the day she was caught the copies she made would have been confiscated, but it sounds like she may have made copies of other files. Where are they?"

"Meow."

"You see it too. The answer has to be in the copies. Thea's house has been gone over on more than one occasion. If there were copies of legal documents someone would have found them. Though I suppose they could have been hidden in an air vent or in a tool box in the garage. Somewhere stealthy."

"Meow."

"Blackmailing is a high-risk activity. If she had proof she wouldn't want to risk it being found. She wouldn't have left it in a drawer or her desk. She would have put the file somewhere no one would think to look."

"Meow."

I stopped walking. "Okay, buddy, it's time to figure this out." I looked out toward the sea as I tried to focus my thoughts. There had to be something I was missing. "Should we go back to Thea's home?"

The cat remained silent. I'd learned in the past that a silent cat meant no. Where else could I look? This case had been complicated because there'd been so much going on at the same time. I needed to think back and remember all the clues the cat had given me.

The first day we met Apollo had led me to Thea's house. When I'd followed him inside he'd been sitting on the desk in front of the stairs. I'd assumed he wanted me to go upstairs and find Thea. The second time he'd led me somewhere it was to see Tansy, but she wasn't there; Bella was. Bella had told us that Tansy was ill, but she'd also shared her vision about the owl. I wondered for the first time if the vision was important to the investigation. Bella had said owl power represented change and intuition. I didn't see how either could help us now.

The next time I followed the cat was back to Thea's home. This time he also led me to the desk. Maybe the desk was the key. I couldn't imagine that Thea had hidden the copies she'd made in her desk and I hadn't seen them, but both times we were in Thea's home Apollo had headed to the desk. That couldn't be a coincidence.

The next time I'd followed Apollo he'd led me to Travis's body, the time after that to the bat that had washed up on shore. I called to Max and turned around and headed back to the cabin. I felt like I was close to some sort of revelation if only I could figure out how everything was connected.

The idea that the desk could be the key stuck with me, so when we returned to the cabin I took out my backpack and dug through it for the things I'd taken from Thea's. There was the small notebook with dates and initials, a two-for-one coupon for Shots, a popular but seedy bar, and a copy of Thea's phone bill. I tossed the phone bill on the table and looked at the notebook. Checking the calendar on my phone, I looked at the dates in the notebook. Every date listed was a Thursday.

I frowned and picked up the coupon. I glanced at Apollo. "I think I know where to look next."

Chapter 15

As I'd sat in my cabin looking through the items I'd taken from Thea's house, I'd realized that not only were all the dates in Thea's notebook Thursdays, but the logo for *late night double shots* included on the coupon was an owl wearing glasses and drinking from a shot glass. Once I had that image in my head, it was a short hop through my memory bank to remember that Jared had said he and Thea had met for drinks every Thursday at Shots.

When I arrived the bar was mostly empty. There were a few people there, but it was early, and Shot's tended to attract a late-night crowd.

"What can I get you?" the bartender asked.

"I just need some information. I understand my friend, Thea Blane, used to come in here on a fairly regular basis."

"Yup. Every Thursday."

"Did she meet anyone?"

"Sometimes. Other times she just picked up someone once she got here. I heard she kicked the can. Too bad. That dame was a real hoot."

"When she came in did she have a favorite place to sit?"

The bartender pointed. "That booth in the corner. If someone was in her seat when she got here she was real quick about kicking them out."

"Maybe I'll have a drink and take a moment to remember her."

The bartender slipped me a draft and I headed across the bar to the booth. Apollo was in the car because I didn't think the bar allowed animals, but I sure wished he was here right now to show me what to do next. Thea had certainly been a more interesting person than I first imagined. On the surface, she was a churchgoing choir member who volunteered at the library, but it seemed her alter ego was a blackmailing trollop with a regular booth in the sleaziest bar in town.

I sat down and looked around. If Thea had hidden something in the bar, where would it be? I ran my hand over the booth bottom and sides but didn't find any sign of a hidden compartment. I bent down and peeked under the table, then sat up and let my eyes scan the walls around me. It would have been almost impossible for Thea to hide something in plain sight of all the other patrons. My instinct was to come to the bar, but suddenly it hit me that Thea's hiding place wasn't a *where* but a *who*.

"Thanks for the drink." I waved at the bartender as I left without having drunk any of the beer.

I got to the car and took out my phone to call Finn. He didn't answer, so I left a message: "Hey,

Finn, it's Cait. I'm at Shots and I think Jared Pitman killed Thea. Not only did the two of them meet here every Thursday, which happens to correspond to the dates on the page in the notebook I found, but I remember him commenting that he hoped we'd catch the person who hit Thea on the back of the head when she wasn't looking. I never told him how Thea died. I just realized I hadn't mentioned it to anyone but the others in the gang. Anyway, unless you told Jared how Thea died, he has to be our guy. Call me back. I'm heading home."

I hung up, took my keys out of my bag, and slipped them into the ignition. I was about to pull away when a man from the bar came running toward me with something in his hand. I rolled down my window and waited.

"Excuse me, but is this your scarf? I found it near the booth where you were sitting."

I glanced at the scarf. "No. It isn't mine, but I appreciate you checking."

"Okay, then." The man turned back toward the bar.

I was about to roll up the window when Apollo leaped across the front seat and out the open window.

"Apollo, you get back here."

The cat ignored me and trotted toward the building. I groaned and opened my door to follow. I thought he was going to go inside the bar, but instead he went around the building toward the alley in the back.

"Come on, kitty. I called Finn and he'll take care of things. Let's go home."

The cat continued to ignore me. He paused at the back door. I slowly made my way toward him, intent on grabbing him, when he jumped up onto a stack of empty boxes set out for disposal.

"Please come down. Tuna for dinner if you do."

"Meow."

I slowly walked toward the boxes, hoping he wouldn't scamper away before I could get to him. He waited until I could almost reach him before he leaped from the boxes and into the building through an open window. I really didn't want to go back into the bar and almost left him. Almost. I whispered a very unladylike word under my breath and climbed up on the boxes, which, fortunately, held my weight. When I was high enough to see inside the window I realized it was the ladies' room. The window wasn't all that big, but I was pretty small, so I grabbed the ledge and slithered through on my belly.

"Okay," I said, looking at the cat. "This had better be good."

The cat jumped up onto the sink. From there, he hopped up onto the top of the stall wall. I tried to see where he was trying to go, but all I could see were a couple of stalls that held toilets and paper supplies, a sink, and a small storage cabinet. I opened the latter, which. contained extra toilet paper and paper towels.

"What?" I asked, holding out my hands in surrender. "I don't know what it is you want me to find."

"Meow." The cat looked up.

I looked up in response. Suddenly, I realized there were fingerprints on one of the ceiling tiles. I pulled the storage cabinet over just a bit and climbed up on it. I pulled back the panel and found a large yellow envelope inside. I pulled it out and looked at Apollo. "I think we just found what we're looking for."

I replaced the ceiling panel and was about to go back out through the window when I heard voices. "Her car is still outside. She must be around here somewhere."

"Do you see her? Because I don't."

"Check the bathroom."

I picked up Apollo, ducked inside one of the stalls, and closed the door. I stood on the toilet so my feet couldn't be seen. I saw a man's feet. He opened the stall next to me. My heart was pounding as I waited for him to find me. Apollo squirmed out of my arms and ran out from under the door.

"What the… Where did you come from?"

The man tried to pick up the cat, who squirted out between his arms.

"What's going on in there?" another man asked.

"There's a cat in here. It must have gotten in through the window."

The second man was standing in the open doorway. Apollo took advantage of that and scooted out the door. Both men took off after him. I used the diversion to go back out through the window. I snuck around the side of the building, but there were men standing in the parking lot between me and my car. I didn't know who I could trust, so I headed into the nearby woods to wait for Finn to rescue me.

Luckily, I didn't have long to wait. I was stepping out from behind the shrubs I was hiding behind when I felt someone grab me from behind.

"Don't make a sound," a male voice said as he put a hand over my mouth.

I nodded.

The next thing I knew, everything went dark.

******

"I'm fine, really," I said to Cody, who was hovering over me.

"Someone hit you hard enough to knock you out. I don't think you're fine."

I put my hand to my head. "It's just a bump. It could have been worse."

"Somehow, the fact that it could have been worse doesn't make me feel any better. I thought we talked about you going off sleuthing on your own."

"I did everything right," I insisted. "Once I figured things out I called Finn and was about to head home when Apollo jumped into the window. Speaking of Apollo, did you find him?"

"Siobhan called. He showed up back at the cabin."

"Back at the cabin? How on earth? You know what, never mind. I'm just glad he's safe. Did Finn arrest Jared?"

"I don't know. He was busy and texted to let me know he'd meet us at the cabin when we're done here."

"When *will* we be done here?"

"As soon as we see the doctor."

I looked around the crowded waiting room and cringed. This wasn't how I wanted to spend my Saturday evening. But as I'd said, it could have been worse. Apollo was okay, I was okay, hopefully Finn had what he needed to arrest Jared, and I had a feeling I was in for at least a week of sympathy foot rubs.

Chapter 16

Sunday, March 18

"Okay, let me get this straight," Maggie said as I tried to explain what she'd missed while she was away. She'd never said when she would be back, but when I headed over to the main house for a cup of coffee early the next morning I'd found her sitting in the kitchen sipping a cup of tea. "First, Tansy told you the cats were leaving the hollow, so you went to investigate, only to find the water had been tainted. On your way out, you found a cat who led you to Thea Blane's body, after which you got caught up in not one but two murders, and this all happened in a matter of days."

"Yup."

"Must have been a busy week."

I smiled. "It was. But in the end things mostly worked out. The group from the university came to treat the water yesterday. It'll take a couple of weeks before it's as crisp and clear as it was, but Tansy is already feeling better and assures me the cats will return. I'm sorry Travis died. I never met him, but I think I might have liked him. Tracking down his killer was bittersweet given the fact that I think at his core Devon wasn't all bad."

"It's hard when the bad guy isn't completely evil."

I took a sip of my coffee before continuing. "It really is, but at least in the case of Jared Pitman I can feel happy he'll spend a good long time in prison. Finn told me the blackmail idea was his. He had some sort of dirt on Thea and coerced her into getting the files he needed. When she had second thoughts he killed her."

"I didn't know Thea well, but I think she was a bit of a lost soul after her divorce," Maggie commented. "She was a good woman at heart, but I suspect she tried so hard to fill the hole in her heart that she made some bad choices. Love can really do a number on you when it goes wrong."

"Speaking of love, how was your trip with Michael?"

A glow came over Maggie's face. "Can I tell you a secret?"

"Of course."

"Michael and I weren't in Hawaii. We were in Ireland."

My eyes grew big. "Ireland? Really? Why all the secrecy?"

"We wanted to return to our ancestral home to marry."

"Marry?" I said a little too loudly.

"Shhh," Maggie said. It was early and the rest of the household was still asleep.

I put my hand over my mouth. "I'm sorry. But wow. You're married?"

Maggie nodded.

"Oh my God." I opened my arms and hugged my favorite aunt. "Congratulations. I'm so happy for you."

Maggie hugged me back. "Thank you. Michael and I are very happy. It was a long time coming but worth the wait."

I wiped a tear from my eye. "I can't believe you finally did it. But, again, why all the secrecy?"

"It was easier this way."

I supposed Maggie had a point. When you fall in love with your high school sweetheart despite the fact that his family had promised him to the church, and then wait more than forty years to be with him while he honors his commitment, I guess things would become complicated.

"Does anyone else know?" I asked.

"No. You're the first. I plan to have the family to dinner this afternoon and make the announcement. I'd appreciate it if you didn't say anything until then."

"Of course. Your secret is safe with me."

"I knew it would be. You kept my other secret for much longer than anyone should have been asked to."

I put my hand over Maggie's and gave it a squeeze. "I love you. Your secrets are always safe with me."

Maggie wiped a tear from her cheek. "There's something else."

"I'm listening."

"Michael and I have decided to move to Puget Sound. We love you all and adore this community, but there will be those who'll never understand why a man who committed his entire life to the church would leave it to marry. We don't want our happiness to be a burden on others or cause dissention within the church."

"Yeah, I guess I get that. And Puget Sound is close. You can come visit all the time."

"Exactly."

"When do you think you'll make the move?"

"Immediately. We have an offer in on a house. We'll stay in a motel until the paperwork goes through. I plan to announce this to the family this afternoon as well, but I wanted to speak to you first. I've decided to give the house to Finn and Siobhan. At one time I indicated I would probably give it to you, but things have changed. Siobhan has moved back to the island, is married, and is starting a family. She needs a nice big house like this for her growing family. And you're engaged to Cody. I know Mr. Parsons made arrangements for his house and land as well as his money to go to Cody when he passes."

"It's fine," I assured Maggie. "I'm sure Siobhan will be thrilled. This house is perfect for them. And while I'm not quite ready to move out of my cabin, I will be getting married and eventually I'll move in with Cody."

"I'm glad you understand. I would have hated it if you felt slighted."

"Not in the least. Really. I've been feeling like the family is going through a transition. You're married and moving away, Finn and Siobhan are having a baby, Cassie is going off to college, and Danny and Aiden are buying a bar."

Maggie raised a brow. "Danny and Aiden are buying a bar?"

"I'll let them tell you about it. And Mom doesn't know yet, so now you have to keep my secret for a few hours."

"I may be moving away, but I'll always keep your secrets as you've kept mine."

I hugged Maggie again. "I'm really going to miss you."

"And I'll miss you all so much."

I paused in response to a noise coming from above. "It sounds like Finn and Siobhan are up. I'll head home so you can talk to them in private. I have to say I'm looking forward to dinner this afternoon. I think it'll be very lively."

"That it will be, my girl. That it will be."

Chapter 17

Monday, March 26

It was just over a week since the team from the university had treated the water, and Tansy and I decided to make a trip into the hollow to check on things. While it was clear not all the cats had returned, we picked up on distant whispers as we walked the steep and rocky trail. Apollo had insisted on coming with us. Normally by this point the cats who show up to help me have moved on to other homes, but my intuition told me Apollo came from the hollow and it was to the hollow he intended to return.

Jared had been arraigned and moved to the larger jail on San Juan Island while he awaited trial. Finn had enough evidence that he felt a jury would put him away for a good long time. Most of the questions we'd set out to answer had been resolved, but I still didn't know who hit me over the head and took the envelope I'd found in the bar ladies' room or what was in it. Sometimes you're forced to live with ambiguity despite your best efforts. I guess this was one of those times, although unanswered questions are never truly dead.

As I looked for the cats along the trail, I knew that although the battle had been won the war might not be over. The water in the hollow had been purified and the cats were returning, but it remained to be seen what would happen when the logging company brought their proposal to the island council. As a strong advocate for the cats, I was confused about where the best answer to the situation lay.

"I understand you'll be visiting New Orleans," Tansy said after a while.

"Yes. In May. Cody's going to be on television to discuss his SEAL training program. Or at least the unclassified parts he can talk about."

"I was wondering if you could do me a favor while you're there."

"Of course. Anything."

"I have a friend, Jasmina. She has something I need. I hoped you could see her to pick it up for me."

"I'd be happy to. I'll just need the address."

"She lives deep in the bayou, so her place isn't easy to find. When you arrive in New Orleans go to the French Quarter. There's a little shop that sells magic supplies. The owner's name is Devalinda. She'll provide you with what you need to navigate the journey to Jasmina's place."

"Okay. Any chance you can tell me what it is I'll be picking up?"

"All in good time."

"Of course."

Our conversation stalled as we continued into the hollow. When we reached the fork in the road we went left, as we had before. When we arrived at the water hole we found a beautiful white cat. Apollo greeted her and started forward. When he was beside the white cat he turned back and meowed. I watched with tears in my eyes as he wandered into the dense forest. I wondered if I'd ever see him again. Most of the cats were gone from my life once the mysteries they had been sent to solve were over, but there were a few I continued to have contact with. I hoped Apollo would be one who would find his way back to me.

I didn't know what the future held, but I was excited to find out. I've learned that life is but a tapestry woven over time. The picture that's revealed will eventually become a representation of my life. Every time I think I know what my tapestry will look like when completed, life throws me a curve, and the image I thought I was weaving turns out to be something else altogether.

Next From Kathi Daley Books

Chapter 1
Sunday, March 25

The first thing I noticed upon entering the room was that the bedspread didn't match the carpet, which was a totally different color than the drapes. Mismatched decor is an odd thing to have float past your consciousness when you've just been told that a man whose friendship you value is dead and your husband is missing. On an intellectual level I knew I was in shock and the emotions that any rational person should and would experience were waiting just below the surface, but in this moment I simply felt nothing.

"Zoe, are you okay?" Sheriff Salinger asked.

I looked away from the drapes and stared at him with what I was sure was a confused expression. I knew something was expected from me, but in that moment I had no idea what it was everyone was waiting for.

"This is too much for her," my friend Levi Denton said. He put his hands on my shoulders, turned my body toward him, and stared into my eyes, a look of concern evident on his face. "She shouldn't be here. There must be another way."

"I don't disagree that it would be best if Zoe didn't need to be here," Salinger said, "but the instructions left by the person or persons who have Zak were very specific."

I averted my eyes from Levi's concerned gaze and looked around the room. There was blood splatter everywhere. My mind began to feel fuzzy as the room seemed to fade in and out. I felt a wave of nausea as I struggled to accept what I'd witnessed with my own eyes. This couldn't be real. It didn't make sense. I put my hand to my face to try to wake myself from this horrible nightmare.

"Zoe?" Levi put a hand on my cheek and gently turned my head so I was looking at him again. He looked so scared. So vulnerable. In that moment I knew this was real and not a dream, as I had hoped. I glanced to the floor and then back to Levi. "How did he die?" I asked as I tried very hard to look away from the outline of Will's body, which had been covered with a sheet.

"Shot in the head," Salinger answered.

I cringed.

"He would have gone quickly, so at least he didn't suffer," Salinger added.

"When?" I asked in a voice so soft that I wondered if anyone had heard.

"The 911 call reporting the sound of a gunshot came through about thirty minutes ago," Salinger answered.

I closed my eyes as a single tear slid down my cheek. Thirty minutes ago, I'd been at home feeding my three-month-old daughter, Catherine Donovan Zimmerman, while Scooter Sherwood and Alex Bremmerton, the two children who lived with Zak and me, chatted about the funny thing they had seen while in town with my parents that afternoon. Thirty minutes ago, I was making plans for the Easter celebration I planned to host the following weekend. Thirty minutes ago I hadn't known that Will was dead or that Zak had been kidnapped by the monster who had killed him.

Levi put his arms around me and pulled me tightly into his chest. I closed my eyes and took comfort in the sound of his strong, steady heartbeat. I knew that giving in to the despair that threatened to overwhelm me wasn't an option. I'd lost a friend today and my heart wanted to weep at the injustice of it. But if the note Salinger held was authentic, Zak was still alive, and it was up to me to save him. I glanced at the sheet on the floor and knew I must set the rage in my soul aside.

"I can take you home if you need some time to process what's happened," Levi offered as I felt my tears soak into his sweater.

I dug down deep for the strength I needed, squeezed him tightly around the waist, and then took a step back. "I'm fine." I turned and looked at Sheriff Salinger. "What do I need to do?"

I knew Salinger had found our friend and employee, Will Danner, lying in a pool of blood after receiving an anonymous 911 call. Will, a teacher at Zimmerman Academy, the private school Zak and I owned, had been staying in a motel near the Academy while his house was being remodeled. Zak had agreed to meet him that evening regarding a project on which they were collaborating. When Salinger arrived, he'd found a note in Will's left hand and a burner cell in his right. The note detailed a very specific set of instructions stating that Zoe Donovan Zimmerman, and only Zoe Donovan Zimmerman, was to call the number provided on the piece of paper with the phone that had been left in Will's hand.

"We need to call the number and find out what they want," Salinger said. "There isn't anything we can do to help Will. What we need to focus on is finding Zak."

I swallowed what felt like a boulder in my throat, "I agree." I held out my hand for the phone. Salinger handed it to me and I looked at it and frowned. "There's blood on it. That doesn't seem right."

"Yeah, there's blood everywhere," Levi said.

"No, Zoe's right," Salinger said, looking at both the phone and the note. Salinger pulled back the sheet, causing me to look away as he did. "There's blood splatter on the phone and the note but not on Will's hands beneath the phone and the note."

"And that's important because…?" Levi asked.

"It's important because it suggests Will was already holding them before he was shot," I explained.

Salinger carefully rolled Will's body to one side and I forced myself to watch. "There isn't any blood beneath his torso," Salinger confirmed.

Levi paled. "Are you telling me some wacko made Will lay on his back holding the phone and note and then shot him in the head?"

"It could have occurred that way, but it's more likely Will was already unconscious when he was shot," Salinger explained.

"I guess that's a good thing," Levi mumbled.

I looked at the phone again. I knew once I started there was no going back. I had no idea where this first phone call would lead, but I had a feeling I was in for a bumpy ride. Nothing else made sense. The setup had been much too elaborate for an easy and painless conclusion to be on the horizon.

I looked at Levi again. He frowned, but I could see he was struggling to be strong for me. "I guess we should do this."

He nodded.

I looked at Salinger. "Are you ready?"

Salinger nodded. "Hold the phone away from your ear so we can hear what's being said as well."

I nodded and pushed the Call button on the phone that had already been programed. After only one ring a deep voice that sounded unreal came on the line. The message seemed to have been prerecorded using an automated voice system.

Welcome to The Sleuthing Game. The purpose of the game is to solve the eight puzzles you will be provided before the allotted time for each runs out. If you are successful, your husband will be returned to you unharmed. If you are unsuccessful you will never see the father of your child alive again. The first set of instructions, as well as the first puzzle, has been taped to the bottom of one of the tables at the Classic Cue pool hall. You have until eight p.m. this evening to retrieve and follow the instructions. No cops or Zak dies.

I glanced at Salinger. "What sort of sicko are we dealing with?"

Salinger frowned. "I don't know."

"It makes no sense that anyone would shoot one man and then kidnap a second one simply to make Zoe engage in a ridiculous game of some sort," Levi stated.

"Do you really think whoever is behind this will kill Zak if I refuse to play?" I asked, fighting the dizziness that threatened to thrust me into a state of unconsciousness. I took a deep breath and fought the urge to slide into the darkness. Focusing on Salinger as he looked around the room, I felt the dizziness dissipate.

"I don't know," he repeated. "But given the fact that he or she has already killed once, I think we have to assume they will."

"Who would do such a thing?" Levi asked a question that had been asked before and I knew would be asked a dozen times more before this was over.

"It's obviously personal," I said as I felt my strength begin to return. "Someone wants to make me jump through a bunch of hoops. I'm going to assume we're dealing with someone I've harmed in the past. The fact that they're referring to their sick ploy as

The Sleuthing Game indicates to me that the person behind this is most likely someone I helped put in jail." I looked at Levi. "I need to do this. I can't risk Zak's life by not cooperating. I need you and Ellie to stay with the kids until this is over."

"You can't do this alone."

"I think I have to. I don't want Ellie and the kids to be alone. I need you to be with them."

I could see Levi wanted to argue, but then Salinger spoke. "I'm going to call the county office to see if I can get a couple of detectives to watch your house."

"Thank you. I'll feel better about things if I know the kids are safe and this psycho can't grab one of them next if that's what they plan." I glanced at my watch. "I need to get a move on if I'm going to find the next set of instructions before the deadline."

"I'll run home and change into plainclothes," Salinger said. "I'll borrow my neighbor's car as well. I'll follow you from a distance."

"What if they see you?" I asked.

"They won't."

"The voice on the phone specifically said no cops," Levi stated. "I know you said you were going to change out of your uniform, but the person who's doing this probably knows what you look like. I think I should be the one to follow Zoe."

I looked toward Levi and shook my head vigorously. "I don't want to put you in any danger. This madman wants me and only me. I need to do this alone."

I couldn't help but notice the look of resolve that crossed Levi's face. "I'm not letting you do this alone. That isn't an option. Someone has to go with you and because the voice on the phone said no cops that someone can't be Salinger."

"But…"

Levi grabbed my shoulders. He forced me to face him. I could see he was as determined to help me as I was for him to be safely out of harm's way. "I'm going with you. I know you don't think you need me, but you do. I know you think you'll be putting me in danger, but you won't. You said yourself this seems to be some sick game between you and whoever is orchestrating it. I doubt they'll have a bit of interest in me."

My resolve hardened. "If it's personal between me and this person why did they kill Will?"

"To get your attention," Levi answered. "To demonstrate the lengths to which they'll go if you don't comply with their instructions. Please." Levi looked me directly in the eye. "I'm going with you. Don't fight me on this."

I glanced at Salinger. "What do you think?"

Salinger shrugged. "I suppose Levi has a good point. You most likely will need help, and as much as I'd like to provide it, maybe he should be the one to go with you. The last thing we want to do is make whoever is behind this angry by ignoring the no-cops dictate. I'll head over to your house and stay with Ellie and the kids until the guys from the county show up. Levi can call me after you retrieve the next set of instructions. I think right now we need to do what the kidnappers are asking to the best of our ability. Once we know what they're really after we can work together to come up with a plan."

"Okay." I looked at Levi, having come to a decision. "Let's go."

The drive between the motel where the attack had occurred and the Classic Cue was accomplished in silence. It took every ounce of strength I could muster not to curl into a fetal position and sob until the sweet peace of unconsciousness overcame me. The thought that Zak was being held by a crazy person filled me with more terror than my mind was able to process and I knew it was only a matter of time before my determination slipped and a feeling of helplessness returned.

I closed my eyes and took a deep breath. I needed to calm my mind so I could focus. I needed to stay strong for Zak. I let my mind wander until eventually it landed on a thought about Catherine and the prebedtime feeding the two of us enjoyed each evening. Catherine knew Ellie and I supposed she would be fine with favorite honorary auntie putting her to bed, but in the three months since she was born I'd never missed a single bedtime feeding.

Given what was going on, it was a good thing I'd been forced to stop breast feeding. I'd felt like a total failure when I learned my body wasn't producing enough of the nutrients my baby needed, but now that I wouldn't be able to be with Catherine for however long this sick, sick game took to complete, I was glad she was used to taking a bottle. It would have been a lot harder on both of us if we hadn't already made the transition.

"We're almost there," Levi said, breaking into my daydream.

I sat up and opened my eyes. "When we get to the Classic Cue I'll go in and find the next set of instructions while you call Ellie. I know Salinger said he was going to head over to the house, but she must be frantic."

"Yeah, I'm sure she probably is."

"Tell her that Alex knows where everything she'll need to take care of Catherine is. And tell her to keep the kids home from school tomorrow. I don't want them to go out at all until we're able to track this guy down and put him safely behind bars."

"Okay. I'll tell her." Levi turned onto the street where the pool hall was located. "Maybe we can figure out who this guy is and where he's holding Zak. If we can find him we can end this. At some point he's bound to make a mistake, give something away."

I glanced out the passenger side window. Familiar buildings passed as we slowly made our way down the street. It was cool this evening, so the sidewalks were sparsely populated; still, it seemed odd that there were people going about their normal lives completely unaware of the fact that Will was dead and Zak was missing. "Yeah," I whispered as Levi stopped at a crosswalk. "We should keep our ears open. The sooner this is over the better."

We arrived at the pool hall and I went in alone. Levi and I weren't certain how the killer would react to his presence, so we decided it was best for him to hang in the background. The pool hall was crowded and the tables were all occupied, which was going to make searching for a note taped beneath one of them difficult. I walked up to the first table, where two men who looked to be in their early twenties were engaged in a game of eight ball. "I'm sorry to interrupt your game, but I need to crawl under your table for just a minute."

"Did you lose something, sweetheart?" one of the men asked after looking me up and down with a suggestive grin on his face.

"I dropped an earring the last time I was here," I lied. "I'll only be a minute."

The men stepped back and I got down on my hands and knees. I tried to ignore the catcalls as I slipped under the table. Yes, I realized my jeans-covered backside was sticking up in the air in a most unfortunate position, but I had little choice in positioning my body as I tried to move around in the tight space. Unfortunately, I didn't find the note, so I thanked the men, then went to the next table and repeated the humiliating process. There were sixteen tables in the room, which would require a lot of time crawling around on the dirty floor with my butt in the air if the note happened to be taped to the last one I checked. Luckily, I found both a note and a cell phone taped to the undercarriage of the eighth table I crawled under. I grabbed both and headed out to the car.

The note contained a set of instructions along with a riddle that, when solved, would lead me to a location. The note indicated that the phone would ring at exactly 9:14. I was to answer it on the third ring. If I had solved the puzzle and ended up in the correct location I would have the information I needed to be able to answer the second question. Once I provided the answer I would be given nine additional minutes to provide five additional answers.

"Okay, so what's the riddle?" Levi asked.

"'To find the clue you must peel back the letters and find that which remains,'" I read aloud.

"Huh?" Levi asked. "What on earth does that mean?"

"I think it's suggesting there's a hidden message contained within the riddle. Or maybe invisible ink was used to write something on the back." I continued to stare at the piece of paper in my hand. The psycho who had gone to all the trouble to orchestrate the game wanted me to play, so they wouldn't have started off with a riddle I couldn't solve.

"Peel back the words," Levi said as he held out his hand, indicating I should give him the note. "Maybe he wants us to focus on part of what's provided. I notice there seem to be a lot of pretty specific numbers."

I thought about the note. The fact that he wanted me to pick up on the third ring and answer the second question was unusual, as was the time of nine-fourteen for the phone call.

"Okay; what numbers are mentioned in order?" I asked. I took out my phone to record them.

"The instructions state that you'll get a call at 9:14, so that's 9-1-4. Then you pick up on the third ring and answer the second question, so that gives us 9-1-4-3-2. After that you'll be given nine minutes to answer five more questions."

"That's 9-1-4-3-2-9-5," I said aloud. 'I know where we need to go."

"Where?" Levi asked.

"It's Zak's private line at Zimmerman Academy."

Recipes

Cranberry Salad—submitted by Pam Curran
Crab Nachos—submitted by Jean Daniel
Cherry Cheese O Cream Pie—submitted by Vivian Shane
Open-faced Apple Plum Cake—submitted by Kristen Pfister

Cranberry Salad

Submitted by Pam Curran

1½ cups fresh cranberries
1 cup water
1 small pkg. lemon Jell-O
1 cup sugar
1 small can crushed pineapple
½ cup chopped nuts
¾ cup chopped celery

Put cranberries and ½ cup water in a saucepan. Cook
on low until berries begin to pop. While the berries
are cooking, boil ½ cup water. Use it to dissolve the
Jell-O. When the berries are done, mix in the
sugar. Combine the cranberries and Jell-O in a
dish. Mix in the remaining ingredients. Place in the
refrigerator until set.

Crab Nachos

Submitted by Jean Daniel

1 lb. lump crabmeat (picked clean)
2 cups tomatillo salsa
1 cup extra sharp grated cheddar cheese
Tortilla chips (I use lime tortilla chips)

Place chips on cookie sheet and heat in a 350-degree oven for 4 minutes. Stir salsa into a pan over medium heat and cook to boiling. Remove from heat and gently fold in crabmeat. Place the tortilla chips in an oven-safe serving plate and spoon the salsa mixture over chips and sprinkle with cheese. Place on middle rack of oven and bake until the cheese bubbles. I garnish with sour cream, black olives, and shredded lettuce.

Cherry Cream O Cheese Pie

Submitted by Vivian Shane

Whenever my mom asked what kind of cake I wanted for my birthday, this pie was always my choice instead. I call it "cheater cheesecake" because it has all the flavor of cheesecake without the hassle of regular cheesecake recipes.

1 8-oz. pkg. cream cheese
1⅓ cups (15-oz. can) sweetened condensed milk
⅓ cup lemon juice
1 tsp. vanilla
1 9″ graham cracker crust
1 can (1 lb. 6 oz) prepared cherry pie filling

Soften cream cheese to room temperature. Whip until fluffy. Gradually add condensed milk, continuing to beat until well blended. Add lemon juice and vanilla; blend well. Pour into crust. Chill 3 hours. Add pie filling to top and serve.

Open-faced Apple or Plum Cake

Submitted by Kristen Pfister

1½ cups sugar (separated into 1 cup and ½ cup)
1 tsp. cinnamon
¼ cup butter (room temperature), plus enough to grease pan
¼ cup margarine (room temperature)
3 eggs
2½ cups flour
2 tsp. baking powder
¼ tsp. salt
½ cup whole milk
 2 tsp. sherry
 3–4 apples peeled and sliced thin (approximately ¼ inch) or 12–14 plums quartered and pitted (do not peel plums)

Optional topping:
1egg
8 oz. sour cream
1 tbs. sugar
½ tsp. cinnamon
10 x 12–15 x ½-inch pan

Preheat oven 375 degrees. Grease pan.
In a separate bowl, combine ½ cup sugar and cinnamon.

Combine butter, margarine, and 1 cup sugar; beat until fluffy

Add one egg at a time, beat thoroughly between each egg.

Add flour, baking powder, salt, milk, and sherry; beat thoroughly.

Turn out batter into pan; spread uniformly.

Firmly press slices into batter.

Sprinkle with sugar and cinnamon mixture.

Bake for approximately 1 hour or until done.

Remove from oven.

If desired, mix egg, sour cream, sugar, and cinnamon and thinly apply to top of cake. Increase oven temp to broil. Place under broiler until topping is slightly golden brown. Remove and let cool.

Books by Kathi Daley

Come for the murder, stay for the romance.

Zoe Donovan Cozy Mystery:
Halloween Hijinks
The Trouble With Turkeys
Christmas Crazy
Cupid's Curse
Big Bunny Bump-off
Beach Blanket Barbie
Maui Madness
Derby Divas
Haunted Hamlet
Turkeys, Tuxes, and Tabbies
Christmas Cozy
Alaskan Alliance
Matrimony Meltdown
Soul Surrender
Heavenly Honeymoon
Hopscotch Homicide
Ghostly Graveyard
Santa Sleuth
Shamrock Shenanigans
Kitten Kaboodle
Costume Catastrophe
Candy Cane Caper
Holiday Hangover
Easter Escapade
Camp Carter
Trick or Treason
Reindeer Roundup
Hippity Hoppity Homicide – *March 2018*

Zimmerman Academy The New Normal
Ashton Falls Cozy Cookbook

Tj Jensen Paradise Lake Mysteries by Henery Press:

Pumpkins in Paradise
Snowmen in Paradise
Bikinis in Paradise
Christmas in Paradise
Puppies in Paradise
Halloween in Paradise
Treasure in Paradise
Fireworks in Paradise
Beaches in Paradise – *July 2018*

Whales and Tails Cozy Mystery:

Romeow and Juliet
The Mad Catter
Grimm's Furry Tail
Much Ado About Felines
Legend of Tabby Hollow
Cat of Christmas Past
A Tale of Two Tabbies
The Great Catsby
Count Catula
The Cat of Christmas Present
A Winter's Tail
The Taming of the Tabby
Frankencat
The Cat of Christmas Future
Farewell to Felines
The Cat of New Orleans – *June 2018*

Writers' Retreat Southern Seashore Mystery:

First Case
Second Look
Third Strike
Fourth Victim
Fifth Night
Sixth Cabin – *May 2018*

Rescue Alaska Paranormal Mystery:

Finding Justice
Finding Answers – *May 2018*

A Tess and Tilly Mystery:

The Christmas Letter
The Valentine Mystery
The Mother's Day Puzzle – *April 2018*

Sand and Sea Hawaiian Mystery:

Murder at Dolphin Bay
Murder at Sunrise Beach
Murder at the Witching Hour
Murder at Christmas
Murder at Turtle Cove
Murder at Water's Edge
Murder at Midnight

Haunting by the Sea:

Homecoming by the Sea – *April 2018*

Seacliff High Mystery:

The Secret
The Curse
The Relic
The Conspiracy
The Grudge
The Shadow
The Haunting

Road to Christmas Romance:

Road to Christmas Past

USA Today best-selling author Kathi Daley lives in beautiful Lake Tahoe with her husband Ken. When she isn't writing, she likes spending time hiking the miles of desolate trails surrounding her home. She has authored more than seventy-five books in eight series, including Zoe Donovan Cozy Mysteries, Whales and Tails Island Mysteries, Sand and Sea Hawaiian Mysteries, Tj Jensen Paradise Lake Series, Writers' Retreat Southern Seashore Mysteries, Rescue Alaska Paranormal Mysteries, and Seacliff High Teen Mysteries. Find out more about her books at **www.kathidaley.com**

Stay up to date:
Newsletter, *The Daley Weekly* **http://eepurl.com/NRPDf**
Kathi Daley Blog – **http://kathidaleyblog.com**
Webpage – **www.kathidaley.com**
Facebook at Kathi Daley Books – **www.facebook.com/kathidaleybooks**
Kathi Daley Books Group Page – **https://www.facebook.com/groups/569578823146850/**
E-mail – **kathidaley@kathidaley.com**
Twitter at Kathi Daley@kathidaley – **https://twitter.com/kathidaley**
Amazon Author Page – **https://www.amazon.com/author/kathidaley**
BookBub – **https://www.bookbub.com/authors/kathi-daley**
Pinterest – **http://www.pinterest.com/kathidaley/**

Made in the USA
San Bernardino, CA
04 April 2018